I

THE EPIC OF

II

ODYSSEUS RETURNS HOME HOMER

III

XERXES INVADES GREECE HERODOTUS

IV

'THE SEA, THE SEA' XENOPHON

V

THE ABDUCTION OF SITA

VI

JASON AND THE GOLDEN FLEECE APOLLONIUS

VII

EXODUS

VIII

THE DESTRUCTION OF TROY VIRGIL

IX

THE SERPENT'S TEETH OVID

X

THE FALL OF JERUSALEM JOSEPHUS

XI

THE MADNESS OF NERO TACITUS

XII

CUPID AND PSYCHE APULEIUS

XIII

THE LEGENDARY ADVENTURES OF ALEXANDER THE GREAT

XIV

BEOWULF

XV

SIEGFRIED'S MURDER

XVI

SAGAS AND MYTHS OF THE NORTHMEN

XVII

THE SUNJATA STORY

XVIII

THE DESCENT INTO HELL DANTE

XIX

KING ARTHUR'S LAST BATTLE MALORY

XX

THE VOYAGES OF SINDBAD

Apuleius

Cupid and Psyche

TRANSLATED BY E. J. KENNEY

PENGUIN EPICS

PENGUIN BOOKS

Published by the Penguin Group
Penguin Books Ltd, 80 Strand, London WC2R ORL, England
Penguin Group (USA) Inc., 375 Hudson Street, New York, New York 10014, USA
Penguin Group (Canada), 90 Eglinton Avenue East, Suite 700, Toronto, Ontario, Canada M4P 2Y3
(a division of Pearson Penguin Canada Inc.)
Penguin Ireland, 25 St Stephen's Green, Dublin 2, Ireland (a division of Penguin Books Ltd)
Penguin Group (Australia), 250 Camberwell Road, Camberwell, Victoria 3124, Australia
(a division of Pearson Australia Group Pty Ltd)
Penguin Books India Pvt Ltd, 11 Community Centre, Panchsheel Park, New Delhi – 110 017, India
Penguin Group (NZ), cnr Airborne and Rosedale Roads, Albany,
Auckland 1310, New Zealand (a division of Pearson New Zealand Ltd)
Penguin Books (South Africa) (Pty) Ltd, 24 Sturdee Avenue,
Rosebank, Johannesburg 2196, South Africa

Penguin Books Ltd, Registered Offices: 80 Strand, London WC2R ORL, England

www.penguin.com

This translation of *The Golden Ass* first published 1998
Revised edition published 2004
This extract published in Penguin Books 2006
1

Translation copyright © E. J. Kenney, 1998, 2004
All rights reserved

The moral right of the translator has been asserted

Typeset by Rowland Phototypesetting Ltd, Bury St Edmunds, Suffolk
Printed in England by Clays Ltd, St Ives plc

ISBN-13: 978-0-141-02637-4
ISBN-10: 0-141-02637-5

Contents

The Story of Cupid and Psyche   1
(from Books IV, V and VI of *The Golden Ass*)

The Golden Ass Book I   47

The Golden Ass Book II   68

Note

The Golden Ass was written in the late second century AD, probably in Carthage (in modern Tunisia), where Apuleius spent a large part of his life. The extracts included here consist of 'The Story of Cupid and Psyche', a story recited by an old woman to a terrified, kidnapped girl and overheard by the narrator (who has been transformed into an ass). This is followed by the opening two books of *The Golden Ass*: these introduce the unfortunate narrator and begin his fabulous adventures.

The Story of Cupid and Psyche

There was once a city with a king and queen who had three beautiful daughters. The two eldest were very fair to see, but not so beautiful that human praise could not do them justice. The loveliness of the youngest, however, was so perfect that human speech was too poor to describe or even praise it satisfactorily. Indeed huge numbers of both citizens and foreigners, drawn together in eager crowds by the fame of such an extraordinary sight, were struck dumb with admiration of her unequalled beauty; and putting right thumb and forefinger to their lips they would offer outright religious worship to her as the goddess Venus. Meanwhile the news had spread through the nearby cities and adjoining regions that the goddess born of the blue depths of the sea and fostered by its foaming waves had made public the grace of her godhead by mingling with mortal men; or at least that, from a new fertilization by drops from heaven, not sea but earth had grown another Venus in the flower of her virginity. And so this belief exceeded all bounds and gained ground day by day, ranging first through the neighbouring islands, then, as the report made its way further afield, through much of the mainland and most of the provinces. Now crowds of people came flocking by long journeys and deep-sea voyages to view this wonder of the age. No one visited Paphos or Cnidos or even Cythera to see the goddess herself; her rites were abandoned, her temples disfigured, her couches trampled, her worship neglected; her statues were ungarlanded, her altars shamefully cold and empty of offerings. It was the girl to whom prayers were addressed, and in human shape that the power of the mighty goddess was placated. When she appeared each morning it was the name of Venus, who was far away, that was propitiated with sacrifices and offerings; and as she walked the streets the people crowded to adore her with garlands and flowers.

This outrageous transference of divine honours to the worship of a mortal girl kindled violent anger in the true Venus, and unable to contain her indignation, tossing her head and protesting in deep bitterness, she thus soliloquized: 'So much for me, the ancient mother of nature, primeval origin of the elements, Venus nurturer of the whole world: I must go halves with a mortal girl in the honour due to my godhead, and my name, established in heaven, is profaned by earthly dirt! It seems that I am to be worshipped in common and that I must put up with the obscurity of being adored by deputy, publicly represented by a girl – a being who is doomed to die! Much good it did me that the shepherd whose impartial fairness was approved by great Jove preferred me for my unrivalled beauty to those great goddesses! But she will rue the day, whoever she is, when she usurped my honours. I'll see to it that she regrets this beauty of hers to which she has no right.'

So saying, she summoned that winged son of hers, that most reckless of creatures, whose wicked behaviour flies in the face of public morals, who armed with torch and arrows roams at night through houses where he has no business, ruining marriages on every hand, committing heinous crimes with impunity, and never doing such a thing as a good deed. Irresponsible as he already was by nature, she aroused him yet more by her words; and taking him to the city and showing him Psyche – this was the girl's name – she laid before him the whole story of this rival beauty. Groaning and crying out in indignation, 'By the bonds of a mother's love,' she said, 'I implore you, by the sweet wounds of your arrows, by the honeyed burns made by your torch, avenge your mother – avenge her to the full. Punish mercilessly that arrogant beauty, and do this one thing willingly for me – it's all I ask. Let this girl be seized with a burning passion for the lowest of mankind, some creature cursed by Fortune in rank, in estate, in condition, someone so degraded that in all the world he can find no wretchedness to equal his own.'

With these words, she kissed her son with long kisses, open-mouthed and closely pressed, and then returned to the nearest point of the seashore. And as she set her rosy feet on the surface of the moving waves, all at once the face of the deep sea became bright and calm. Scarcely had she formed the wish when immediately, as if she had previously ordered it, her marine entourage was prompt to appear. There came the daughters of Nereus singing in harmony, Portunus with his thick sea-green beard, Salacia, the folds of her robe heavy with fish, and little Palaemon astride his dolphin. On all sides squadrons of Tritons cavorted over the sea. One softly sounded his loud horn, a second with a silken veil kept off the heat of her enemy the Sun, a third held his mistress's mirror before

her face, and others yoked in pairs swam beneath her car.
Such was the retinue that escorted Venus in her progress
to Ocean.

Psyche meanwhile, for all her striking beauty, had no
joy of it. Everyone feasted their eyes on her, everyone
praised her, but no one, king, prince, or even commoner,
came as a suitor to ask her in marriage. Though all
admired her divine loveliness, they did so merely as one
admires a statue finished to perfection. Long ago her
two elder sisters, whose unremarkable looks had enjoyed
no such widespread fame, had been betrothed to royal
suitors and achieved rich marriages; Psyche stayed at
home an unmarried virgin mourning her abandoned and
lonely state, sick in body and mind, hating this beauty of
hers which had enchanted the whole world. In the end
the unhappy girl's father, sorrowfully suspecting that the
gods were offended and fearing their anger, consulted
the most ancient oracle of Apollo at Miletus, and implored the great god with prayers and sacrifices to grant
marriage and a husband to his slighted daughter. But
Apollo, though Greek and Ionian, in consideration for
the writer of a Milesian tale, replied in Latin:

> On mountain peak, O King, expose the maid
>   For funeral wedlock ritually arrayed.
> No human son-in-law (hope not) is thine,
>   But something cruel and fierce and serpentine;
> That plagues the world as, borne aloft on wings,
>   With fire and steel it persecutes all things;
> That Jove himself, he whom the gods revere,
>   That Styx's darkling stream regards with fear.

The king had once accounted himself happy; now, on hearing the utterance of the sacred prophecy, he returned home reluctant and downcast, to explain this inauspicious reply, and what they had to do, to his wife. There followed several days of mourning, of weeping, of lamentation. Eventually the ghastly fulfilment of the terrible oracle was upon them. The gear for the poor girl's funereal bridal was prepared; the flame of the torches died down in black smoke and ash; the sound of the marriage-pipe was changed to the plaintive Lydian mode; the joyful marriage-hymn ended in lugubrious wailings; and the bride wiped away her tears with her own bridal veil. The whole city joined in lamenting the sad plight of the afflicted family, and in sympathy with the general grief all public business was immediately suspended.

However, the bidding of heaven had to be obeyed, and the unfortunate Psyche was required to undergo the punishment ordained for her. Accordingly, amid the utmost sorrow, the ceremonies of her funeral marriage were duly performed, and escorted by the entire populace Psyche was led forth, a living corpse, and in tears joined in, not her wedding procession, but her own funeral. While her parents, grief-stricken and stunned by this great calamity, hesitated to complete the dreadful deed, their daughter herself encouraged them: 'Why do you torture your unhappy old age with prolonged weeping? Why do you weary your spirit – my spirit rather – with constant cries of woe? Why do you disfigure with useless tears the faces which I revere? Why by tearing your eyes do you tear mine? Why do you pull out your white hairs? Why do you beat your breasts, those breasts which to me are holy? These, it seems, are the glorious rewards for you of my incomparable beauty. Only now is it given to you to understand that it is wicked Envy that has dealt you this deadly blow. Then, when nations and peoples were paying us divine honours, when with one voice they were hailing me as a new Venus, that was when you should have grieved, when you should have wept, when you should have mourned me as already lost. Now I too understand, now I see that it is by the name of Venus alone that I am destroyed. Take me and leave me on the rock to which destiny has assigned me. I cannot wait to enter on this happy marriage, and to see that noble bridegroom of mine. Why should I postpone, why should I shirk my meeting with him who is born for the ruin of the whole world?'

After this speech the girl fell silent, and with firm step she joined the escorting procession. They came to the prescribed crag on the steep mountain, and on the top-most summit they set the girl and there they all aban-doned her; leaving there too the wedding torches with which they had lighted their path, extinguished by their tears, with bowed heads they took their way homeward. Psyche's unhappy parents, totally prostrated by this great calamity, hid themselves away in the darkness of their shuttered palace and abandoned themselves to perpetual night. Her, however, fearful and trembling and lament-ing her fate there on the summit of the rock, the gentle breeze of softly breathing Zephyr, blowing the edges of her dress this way and that and filling its folds, impercep-tibly lifted up; and carrying her on his tranquil breath

smoothly down the slope of the lofty crag he gently let
her sink and laid her to rest on the flowery turf in the
bosom of the valley that lay below.

In this soft grassy spot Psyche lay pleasantly reclining
on her bed of dewy turf and, her great disquiet of mind
soothed, fell sweetly asleep. Presently, refreshed by a
good rest, she rose with her mind at ease. What she now
saw was a park planted with big tall trees and a spring
of crystal-clear water. In the very centre of the garden,
by the outflow of the spring, a palace had been built, not
by human hands but by a divine craftsman. Directly
you entered you knew that you were looking at the
pleasure-house of some god – so splendid and delightful
it was. For the coffering of the ceiling was of citron-wood
and ivory artfully carved, and the columns supporting it
were of gold; all the walls were covered in embossed
silver, with wild beasts and other animals confronting
the visitor on entering. Truly, whoever had so skilfully
imparted animal life to all that silver was a miracle-
worker or a demigod or indeed a god! Furthermore,
the very floors were divided up into different kinds of
pictures in mosaic of precious stones: twice indeed and
more than twice marvellously happy those who walk
on gems and jewellery! As far and wide as the house
extended, every part of it was likewise of inestimable
price. All the walls, which were built of solid blocks of
gold, shone with their own brilliance, so that the house
furnished its own daylight, sun or no sun; such was the
radiance of the rooms, the colonnades, the very doors.
The rest of the furnishings matched the magnificence of
the building, so that it would seem fair to say that great

Jove had built himself a heavenly palace to dwell among mortals.

Drawn on by the delights of this place, Psyche approached and, becoming a little bolder, crossed the threshold; then, allured by her joy in the beautiful spectacle, she examined all the details. On the far side of the palace she discovered lofty storehouses crammed with rich treasure; there is nothing that was not there. But in addition to the wonder that such wealth could exist, what was most astonishing was that this vast treasure of the entire world was not secured by a single lock, bolt, or guard. As she gazed at all this with much pleasure there came to her a disembodied voice: 'Mistress, you need not be amazed at this great wealth. All of it is yours. Enter then your bedchamber, sleep off your fatigue, and go to your bath when you are minded. We whose voices you hear are your attendants who will diligently wait on you; and when you have refreshed yourself a royal banquet will not be slow to appear for you.' Psyche recognized her happy estate as sent by divine Providence, and obeying the instructions of the bodiless voice she dispelled her weariness first with sleep and then with a bath. There immediately appeared before her a semicircular seat; seeing the table laid she understood that this provision was for her entertainment and gladly took her place. Instantly course after course of wine like nectar and of different kinds of food was placed before her, with no servant to be seen but everything wafted as it were on the wind. She could see no one but merely heard the words that were uttered, and her waiting maids were nothing but voices to her. When the rich feast was over, there entered an invisible singer, and another performed on a lyre, itself invisible. This was succeeded by singing in concert, and though not a soul was to be seen, there was evidently a whole choir present.

These pleasures ended, at the prompting of dusk Psyche went to bed. Night was well advanced when she heard a gentle sound. Then, all alone as she was and fearing for her virginity, Psyche quailed and trembled, dreading, more than any possible harm, the unknown. Now there entered her unknown husband; he had mounted the bed, made her his wife, and departed in haste before sunrise. At once the voices that were in waiting in the room ministered to the new bride's slain virginity. Things went on in this way for some little time; and, as is usually the case, the novelty of her situation became pleasurable to her by force of habit, while the sound of the unseen voice solaced her solitude.

Meanwhile her parents were pining away with ceaseless grief and sorrow; and as the news spread her elder sisters learned the whole story. Immediately, sad and downcast, they left home and competed with each other in their haste to see and talk to their parents. That night her husband spoke to Psyche – for though she could not see him, her hands and ears told her that he was there – as follows: 'Sweetest Psyche, my dear wife, Fortune in yet more cruel guise threatens you with mortal danger: I charge you to be most earnestly on your guard against it. Your sisters, believing you to be dead, are now in their grief following you to the mountain-top and will soon be there. If you should hear their lamentations, do not answer or even look that way, or you will bring about heavy grief for me and for yourself sheer destruction.' She agreed and promised to do her husband's bidding, but as soon as he and the night had vanished together, the unhappy girl spent the whole day crying and mourning, constantly repeating that now she was utterly destroyed: locked up in this rich prison and deprived of intercourse or speech with human beings, she could not bring comfort to her sisters in their sorrow or even set eyes on them. Unrevived by bath or food or any other refreshment and weeping inconsolably she retired to rest.

It was no more than a moment before her husband, earlier than usual, came to bed and found her still in tears. Taking her in his arms he remonstrated with her: 'Is this what you promised, my Psyche? I am your husband: what am I now supposed to expect from you? What am I supposed to hope? All day, all night, even in your husband's arms, you persist in tormenting yourself. Do then as you wish and obey the ruinous demands of your heart. Only be mindful of my stern warning when – too late – you begin to be sorry.' Then with entreaties and threats of suicide she forced her husband to agree to her wishes: to see her sisters, to appease their grief, to talk with them. So he yielded to the prayers of his new bride, and moreover allowed her to present them with whatever she liked in the way of gold or jewels, again and again, however, repeating his terrifying warnings: she must never be induced by the evil advice of her sisters to discover what her husband looked like, or allow impious curiosity to hurl her down to destruction from the heights on which Fortune had placed her, and so for ever deprive her of his embraces. Psyche thanked her husband and, happier now in her mind, 'Indeed,' she said, 'I will die a hundred deaths before I let myself be robbed of this most delightful marriage with you. For I love and adore you to distraction, whoever you are, as I love my own life; Cupid himself cannot compare with you. But this too I beg you to grant me: order your servant Zephyr to bring my sisters to me as he brought me here' – and planting seductive kisses, uttering caressing words, and entwining him in her enclosing arms, she added to her endearments 'My darling, my husband, sweet soul of your Psyche.' He unwillingly gave way under the powerful influence of her murmured words of love, and promised to do all she asked; and then, as dawn was now near, he vanished from his wife's arms.

The sisters inquired the way to the rock where Psyche had been left and hurriedly made off to it, where they started to cry their eyes out and beat their breasts, so that the rocky crags re-echoed their ceaseless wailings. They went on calling their unhappy sister by name, until the piercing noise of their shrieks carried down the mountainside and brought Psyche running out of the palace in distraction, crying: 'Why are you killing your-selves with miserable lamentation for no reason? I whom you are mourning, I am here. Cease your sad outcry, dry now your cheeks so long wet with tears; for now you can embrace her for whom you were grieving.' Then she summoned Zephyr and reminded him of her husband's order. On the instant he obeyed her command and on his most gentle breeze at once brought them to her unharmed. Then they gave themselves over to the enjoyment of embraces and eager kisses; and coaxed by their joy the tears which they had restrained now broke out again. 'But now,' said Psyche, 'enter in happiness my house and home and with your sister restore your tormented souls.' With these words she showed them the great riches of the golden palace and let them listen to the retinue of slave-voices, and refreshed them sumptuously with a luxurious bath and the supernatural splendours of her table. They, having enjoyed to the full this profusion of divine riches, now began deep in their hearts to cherish envy. Thus one of them persisted with minute inquiries, asking who was the master of this heavenly household and who or what was Psyche's husband. Psyche, however, scrupulously respected her husband's orders and did not allow herself to forget them; she improvised a story that he was a handsome young man whose beard had only just begun to grow and that he spent most of his time farming or hunting in the mountains. Then, fearing that if the conversation went on too long some slip would give away her secret thoughts, she loaded them with gold plate and jewellery, immediately summoned Zephyr, and handed them over to him for their return journey.

No sooner said than done. The worthy sisters on their return home were now inflamed by the poison of their growing envy, and began to exchange vociferous complaints. So then the first started: 'You see the blindness, the cruelty and injustice of Fortune! – content, it would seem, that sisters of the same parents should fare so differently. Here are we, the elder sisters, handed over to foreign husbands as slaves, banished from our home, our own country, to live the life of exiles far from our parents, while she, the youngest, the offspring of a late birth from a worn-out womb, enjoys huge wealth and a god for husband. Why, she doesn't even know how to make proper use of all these blessings. You saw, sister, all the priceless necklaces, the resplendent stuffs, the sparkling gems, the gold everywhere underfoot. If this husband of hers is as handsome as she says, she is the happiest woman alive. Perhaps, though, as he learns to know her and his love is strengthened, her god-husband will make her a goddess too. Yes, yes, that's it: that explains her behaviour and her attitude. She's already looking to heaven and fancying herself a goddess, this woman who has voices for slaves and lords it over the winds themselves. And I, God help me, am fobbed off with a husband older than my father, bald as a pumpkin and puny as a child, who keeps the whole house shut up with bolts and bars.'

Her sister took up the refrain: 'And I have to put up with a husband bent double with rheumatism and so hardly ever able to give me what a woman wants. I'm always having to massage his twisted, stone-hard fingers, spoiling these delicate hands of mine with stinking compresses and filthy bandages and loathsome plasters – so that it's not a dutiful wife I look like but an overworked sick-nurse. You must decide for yourself, sister, how patiently – or rather slavishly, for I shall say frankly what I think – you can bear this; as for me, I can no longer stand the sight of such good fortune befalling one so unworthy of it. Do you remember the pride, the arrogance, with which she treated us? How her boasting, her shame-less showing off, revealed her puffed-up heart? With what bad grace she tossed us a few scraps of her vast wealth and then without more ado, tiring of our company, ordered us to be thrust – blown – whistled away? As I'm a woman, as sure as I stand here, I'll hurl her down to ruin from her great riches. And if you too, as you have every right to do, have taken offence at her contemptuous treatment of us, let us put our heads together to devise strong measures. Let us not show these presents to our parents or to anybody else, and let us pretend not to know even whether she is alive or dead. It's enough that we've seen what we wish we hadn't, without spreading this happy news of her to them and to the rest of the world. You aren't really rich if nobody knows that you are. She is going to find out that she has elder sisters, not servants. Now let us return to our husbands and go back to our homes – poor but decent – and then when we've thought things over seriously let us equip ourselves with an even firmer resolve to punish her insolence.'

The two evil women thought well of this wicked plan, and having hidden all their precious gifts, they tore their hair and clawed their cheeks (no more than they deserved), renewing their pretence of mourning. In this way they inflamed their parents' grief all over again; and then, taking a hasty leave of them, they made off to their homes swollen with mad rage, to devise their wicked – their murderous – plot against their innocent sister. Meanwhile Psyche's mysterious husband once more warned her as they talked together that night: 'Don't you see the danger that threatens you? Fortune is now engaging your outposts, and if you do not stand very firmly on your guard she will soon be grappling with you hand to hand. These treacherous she-wolves are doing their best to lay a horrible trap for you; their one aim is to persuade you to try to know my face – but if you do see it, as I have constantly told you, you will not see it. So then if those vile witches come, as I know they will, armed with their deadly designs, you must not even talk to them; but if because of your natural lack of guile and tenderness of heart you are unequal to that, at least you must refuse to listen to or answer any questions about your husband. For before long we are going to increase our family; your womb, until now a child's, is carrying a child for us in its turn – who, if you hide our secret in silence, will be divine, but if you divulge it, he will be mortal.' Hearing this, Psyche, blooming with happiness, clapped her hands at the consoling thought of a divine child, exulting in the glory of this pledge that was to come and rejoicing in the dignity of being called a mother. Anxiously she counted the growing tale of days and months as they passed, and as she learned to bear her unfamiliar burden she marvelled that from a moment's pain there should come so fair an increase of her rich womb.

But now those plagues, foulest Furies, breathing viperine poison and pressing on in their devilish haste, had started their voyage; and once more her transitory husband warned Psyche: 'The day of reckoning and the last chance are here. Your own sex, your own flesh and blood, are the enemy, arrayed in arms against you; they have marched out and drawn up their line, and sounded the trumpet-call; with drawn sword your abominable sisters are making for your throat. What disasters press upon us, sweetest Psyche! Have pity on yourself and on us both; remember your duty and control yourself, save your home, your husband, and this little son of ours from the catastrophe that threatens us. You cannot call those wicked women sisters any longer; in their murderous hatred they have spurned the ties of blood. Do not look at them, do not listen to them, when like the Sirens aloft on their crag they make the rocks ring with their deadly voices.'

As she replied, Psyche's voice was muffled by sobs and tears: 'More than once, I know, you have put my loyalty and discretion to the proof, but none the less now you shall approve my strength of mind. Only once more order our Zephyr to do his duty, and instead of your own sacred face that is denied me let me at least behold my sisters. By those fragrant locks that hang so abundantly, by those soft smooth cheeks so like mine, by that breast warm with hidden heat, as I hope to see your face at least in this little one: be swayed by the dutiful prayers of an anxious suppliant, allow me to enjoy my sisters' embrace, and restore and delight the soul of your devoted Psyche. As to your face, I ask nothing more; even the darkness of night does not blind me; I have you as my light.' Enchanted by her words and her soft embrace, her husband dried her tears with his hair, promised to do as she asked, and then left at once just as day was dawning.

The two sisters, sworn accomplices, without even

visiting their parents, disembarked and made their way at breakneck speed straight to the well-known rock, where, without waiting for their conveying wind to appear, they launched themselves with reckless daring into the void. However, Zephyr, heeding though reluctantly his royal master's commands, received them in the embrace of his gentle breeze and brought them to the ground. Without losing a second they immediately marched into the palace in close order, and embracing their victim these women who belied the name of sister, hiding their rich store of treachery under smiling faces, began to fawn on her: 'Psyche, not little Psyche any longer, so you too are a mother! Only fancy what a blessing for us you are carrying in your little pocket! Think of the joy and gladness for our whole house! Imagine what pleasure we shall take in raising this marvellous child! If he is, as he ought to be, as fair as his parents, it will be a real Cupid that will be born.'

With such pretended affection did they little by little make their way into their sister's heart. Then and there she sat them down to recover from the fatigues of their journey, provided warm baths for their refreshment, and then at table entertained them splendidly with all those wonderful rich eatables and savoury delicacies of hers. She gave an order, and the lyre played; another, and there was pipe-music; another, and the choir sang. All these invisible musicians soothed with their sweet strains the hearts of the listeners. Not that the malice of the wicked sisters was softened or quieted even by the honeyed sweetness of the music; directing their conversation towards the trap their guile had staked out they craftily began to ask Psyche about her husband, his family, his class, his occupation. She, silly girl that she was, forgetting what she had said before, concocted a new story and told them that her husband was a prosperous merchant from the neighbouring province, a middle-aged man with a few white hairs here and there. However, she did not dwell on this for more than a moment or two, but again returned them to their aerial transport loaded with rich gifts.

No sooner were they on their way back, carried aloft by Zephyr's calm breath, than they began to hold forth to each other: 'Well, sister, what is one to say about that silly baggage's fantastic lies? Last time it was a youth with a fluffy beard, now it's a middle-aged man with white hair. Who is this who in a matter of days has been suddenly transformed into an old man? Take it from me, sister, either the little bitch is telling a pack of lies or she doesn't know what her husband looks like. Whichever it is, she must be relieved of those riches of hers without more ado. If she doesn't know his shape, obviously it is a god she has married and it's a god her pregnancy will bring us. All I can say is, if she's called – God forbid – the mother of a divine child, I'll hang myself and be done with it. Meanwhile then let us go back to our parents, and we'll patch together the most colourable fabrication we can to support what we've agreed on.'

On fire with this idea they merely greeted their parents in passing; and having spent a disturbed and wakeful night, in the morning they flew to the rock. Under the protection as usual of the wind they swooped down in a fury, and rubbing their eyelids to bring on the tears they craftily accosted the girl: 'There you sit, happy and blessed in your very ignorance of your misfortune and careless of your danger, while we can't sleep for watching over your welfare, and are suffering acute torments in your distress. For we know for a fact, and you know we share all your troubles and misfortunes, so we cannot hide it from you, that it is an immense serpent, writhing its knotted coils, its bloody jaws dripping deadly poison, its maw gaping deep, if only you knew it, that sleeps with you each night. Remember now the Pythian oracle, which gave out that you were fated to wed a wild beast. Many peasants and hunters of the region and many of your neighbours have seen him coming back from feeding and bathing in the waters of the nearby river. They all say that it won't be for long that he will go on fattening you so obligingly, but that as soon as the fullness of your womb brings your pregnancy to maturity and you are that much more rich and enjoyable a prize, he will eat you up. Well, there it is; it's you who must decide whether to take the advice of your sisters who are worried for your life, and escape death by coming to live in safety with us, or be entombed in the entrails of a savage monster. However, if a country life and musical solitude, and the loathsome and dangerous intimacy of clandestine love, and the embraces of a venomous serpent, are what appeals to you, at all events your loving sisters will have done their duty.'

Then poor Psyche, simple and childish creature that she was, was seized by fear at these grim words. Beside herself, she totally forgot all her husband's warnings and her own promises, and hurled herself headlong into an abyss of calamity. Trembling, her face bloodless and ghastly, she scarcely managed after several attempts to whisper from half-opened lips: 'Dearest sisters, you never fail in your loving duty, as is right and proper, and I do not believe that those who have told you these things are lying. For I have never seen my husband's face and I have no idea where he comes from; only at night, obeying his voice, do I submit to this husband of unknown condition – one who altogether shuns the light; and when you say that he must be some sort of wild beast, I can only agree with you. For he constantly terrifies me with warnings not to try to look at him, and threatens me with a fearful fate if I am curious about his appearance. So if you can offer some way of escape to your sister in her peril, support her now: for if you desert me at this point, all the benefits of your earlier concern will be lost.'

The gates were now thrown open, and these wicked women stormed Psyche's defenceless heart; they ceased sapping and mining, drew the swords of their treachery, and attacked the panic-stricken thoughts of the simple-minded girl. First one began: 'Since the ties of blood forbid us to consider danger when your safety is at stake, let us show you the only way that can save you, one that we have long planned. Take a very sharp blade and give it an additional edge by stropping it gently on your palm, then surreptitiously hide it on your side of the bed; get ready a lamp and fill it with oil, then when it is burning brightly put it under cover of a jar of some kind, keeping all these preparations absolutely secret; and then, when he comes, leaving his furrowed trail behind him, and mounts the bed as usual, as he lies outstretched and, enfolded in his first heavy sleep, begins to breathe deeply, slip out of bed and with bare feet taking tiny steps one by one on tiptoe, free the lamp from its prison of blind darkness; and consulting the light as to the best moment for your glorious deed, with that two-edged weapon, boldly, first raising high your right hand, with powerful stroke, there where the deadly serpent's head and neck are joined – cut them apart. Our help will not be wanting; the instant you have secured yourself by his death, we shall be anxiously awaiting the moment to fly to you; then we will take all these riches back along with you and make a desirable marriage for you, human being to human being.'

Their sister had been on fire; these words kindled her heart to a fierce flame. They immediately left her, fearing acutely to be found anywhere near such a crime. Carried back as usual on the wings of the wind and deposited on the rock, they at once made themselves scarce, embarked, and sailed away. But Psyche, alone now except for the savage Furies who harried her, was tossed to and fro in her anguish like the waves of the sea. Though she had taken her decision and made up her mind, now that she came to put her hand to the deed she began to waver, unsure of her resolve, torn by the conflicting emotions of her terrible situation. Now she was eager, now she would put it off; now she dared, now she drew back; now she was in despair, now in a rage; and, in a word, in one and the same body she loathed the monster and loved the husband. However, when evening ushered in the night, she hurried to prepare for her dreadful deed.

Night came, and with it her husband, who, having first engaged on the field of love, fell into a deep sleep.

Then Psyche, though naturally weak in body, rallied her strength with cruel Fate reinforcing it, produced the lamp, seized the blade, and took on a man's courage. But as soon as the light was brought out and the secret of their bed became plain, what she saw was of all wild beasts the most soft and sweet of monsters, none other than Cupid himself, the fair god fairly lying asleep. At the sight the flame of the lamp was gladdened and flared up, and her blade began to repent its blasphemous edge. Psyche, unnerved by the wonderful vision, was no longer mistress of herself: feeble, pale, trembling and powerless, she crouched down and tried to hide the steel by burying it in her own bosom; and she would certainly have done it, had not the steel in fear of such a crime slipped and flown out of her rash hands. Now, overcome and utterly lost as she was, yet as she gazed and gazed on the beauty of the god's face, her spirits returned. She saw a rich head of golden hair dripping with ambrosia, a milk-white neck, and rosy cheeks over which there strayed coils of hair becomingly arranged, some hanging in front, some behind, shining with such extreme brilliance that the lamplight itself flickered uncertainly. On the shoulders of the flying god there sparkled wings, dewy-white with glistening sheen, and though they were at rest the soft delicate down at their edges quivered and rippled in incessant play. The rest of the god's body was smooth and shining and such as Venus need not be ashamed of in her son. At the foot of the bed lay a bow, a quiver, and arrows, the gracious weapons of the great god.

Curious as ever, Psyche could not restrain herself from examining and handling and admiring her husband's weapons. She took one of the arrows out of the quiver and tried the point by pricking her thumb; but as her hands were still trembling she used too much force, so that the point went right in and tiny drops of blood bedewed her skin. Thus without realizing it Psyche through her own act fell in love with Love. Then ever more on fire with desire for Desire she hung over him gazing in distraction and devoured him with quick sensuous kisses, fearing all the time that he might wake up. Carried away by joy and sick with love, her heart was in turmoil; but meanwhile that wretched lamp, either through base treachery, or in jealous malice, or because it longed itself to touch such beauty and as it were to kiss it, disgorged from its spout a drop of hot oil on to the right shoulder of the god. What! Rash and reckless lamp, lowly instrument of love, to burn the lord of universal fire himself, when it must have been a lover who first invented the lamp so that he could enjoy his desires for even longer at night! The god, thus burned, leapt up, and seeing his confidence betrayed and sullied, flew off from the loving embrace of his unhappy wife without uttering a word.

But as he rose Psyche just managed to seize his right leg with both hands, a pitiful passenger in his lofty flight; trailing attendance through the clouds she clung on underneath, but finally in her exhaustion fell to the ground. Her divine lover did not abandon her as she lay there, but alighting in a nearby cypress he spoke to her from its lofty top with deep emotion: 'Simple-minded

Psyche, forgetting the instructions of my mother Venus, who ordered that you should be bound by desire for the lowest of wretches and enslaved to a degrading marriage, I myself flew to you instead as your lover. But this I did, I know, recklessly; I, the famous archer, wounded myself with my own weapons and made you my wife – so that, it seems, you might look on me as a monster and cut off this head which carries these eyes that love you. This is what I again and again advised you to be always on your guard against; this is what I repeatedly warned of in my care for you. But those worthy counsellors of yours shall speedily pay the price of their pernicious teaching; your punishment shall merely be that I shall leave you.' And with these last words he launched himself aloft on his wings.

Psyche, as she lay and watched her husband's flight for as long as she could see him, grieved and lamented bitterly. But when with sweeping wings he had soared away and she had altogether lost sight of him in the distance, she threw herself headlong off the bank of a nearby stream. But the gentle river, in respect it would seem for the god who is wont to scorch even water, and fearing for himself, immediately bore her up unharmed on his current and landed her on his grassy bank. It happened that the country god Pan was sitting there with the mountain nymph Echo in his arms, teaching her to repeat all kinds of song. By the bank his kids browsed and frolicked at large, cropping the greenery of the river. The goat-god, aware no matter how of her plight, called the lovesick and suffering Psyche to him kindly and caressed her with soothing words: 'Pretty child, I may be a rustic and a herdsman, but age and experience have taught me a great deal. If I guess aright – and this indeed is what learned men style divination – from these tottering and uncertain steps of yours, and from your deathly pallor, and from your continual sighing, and from your swimming eyes, you are desperately in love. Listen to me then, and do not try to destroy yourself again by jumping off heights or by any other kind of unnatural death. Stop weeping and lay aside your grief; rather adore in prayer Cupid, greatest of gods, and strive to earn his favour, young wanton and pleasure-loving that he is, through tender service.'

These were the words of the herdsman-god. Psyche made no reply, but having worshipped his saving power went on her way. But when she had wandered far and wide with toilsome steps, as day waned she came without realizing it by a certain path to the city where the husband of one of her sisters was king. On discovering this, Psyche had herself announced to her sister. She was ushered in, and after they had exchanged greetings and embraces she was asked why she had come. Psyche replied: 'You remember the advice you both gave me, how you persuaded me to kill with two-edged blade the monster who slept with me under the false name of husband, before he swallowed me up, poor wretch, in his greedy maw. I agreed; but as soon as with the conniving light I set eyes on his face, I saw a wonderful, a divine spectacle, the son of Venus himself, I mean Cupid, deeply and peacefully asleep. But as I was thrilling to the glorious sight, overwhelmed with pleasure but in anguish because I was powerless to enjoy it, by the unhappiest of chances the lamp spilt a drop of boiling oil on to his shoulder. Aroused instantly from sleep by the pain, and seeing me armed with steel and flame, "For this foul crime," he said, "leave my bed this instant and take your chattels with you. I shall wed your sister" – and he named you – "in due form." And immediately he ordered Zephyr to waft me outside the boundaries of his palace.'

Before Psyche had finished speaking, her sister, stung by frantic lust and malignant jealousy, concocted on the spot a story to deceive her husband, to the effect that she had had news of her parents' death, and immediately took ship and hurried to the well-known rock. There, though the wind was blowing from quite a different quarter, yet besotted with blind hope she cried: 'Receive me, Cupid, a wife worthy of you, and you, Zephyr, bear up your mistress', and with a mighty leap threw herself over. But not even in death did she reach the place she sought: for as she fell from one rocky crag to another she was torn limb from limb, and she died providing a banquet of her mangled flesh, as she so richly deserved, for the birds of prey and wild beasts. The second vengeance soon followed. For Psyche again in her wanderings arrived at another city, where her second sister likewise lived. She too was no less readily taken in by her sister's ruse, and eager to supplant her in an unhallowed marriage she hurried off to the rock and fell to a similar death.

Meanwhile, as Psyche was scouring the earth, bent on her search for Cupid, he lay groaning with the pain of the burn in his mother's chamber. At this point a tern, that pure white bird which skims over the sea-waves in its flight, plunged down swiftly to the very bottom of the sea. There sure enough was Venus bathing and swimming; and perching by her the bird told her that her son had been burned and lay suffering from the sharp pain of his wound and in peril of his life. Now throughout the whole world the good name of all Venus' family was besmirched by all kinds of slanderous reports. People were saying: 'He has withdrawn to whoring in the mountains, she to swimming in the sea; and so there is no pleasure anywhere, no grace, no charm, everything is rough, savage, uncouth. There are no more marriages, no more mutual friendships, no children's love, nothing but endless squalor and repellent, distasteful, and sordid couplings.' Such were the slanders this garrulous and meddlesome bird whispered in Venus' ear to damage her son's honour. Venus was utterly furious and exclaimed: 'So then, this worthy son of mine has a mistress? You're the only servant I have that I can trust: out with it, the name of this creature who has debauched a simple childish boy – is it one of the tribe of the Nymphs, or one of the number of the Hours, or one of the choir of the Muses, or one of my attendant Graces?' The voluble bird answered promptly: 'I do not know, my lady; but I think it's a girl called Psyche, if I remember rightly, whom he loves to distraction.' Venus, outraged, cried out loud: 'Psyche is it, my rival in beauty, the usurper of my name, whom he loves? Really? I suppose my lord took me for a go-between to introduce him to the girl?'

Proclaiming her wrongs in this way she hurriedly left the sea and went at once to her golden bedchamber, where she found her ailing son as she had been told. Hardly had she passed through the door when she started to shout at him: 'Fine goings-on, these, a credit to our family and your character for virtue! First you ride rough-shod over your mother's – no, your sovereign's – orders, by not tormenting my enemy with a base amour; then you, a mere child, actually receive her in your vicious adolescent embraces, so that I have to have my enemy as my daughter-in-law. I suppose you think, you odious good-for-nothing lecher, that you're the only one fit to breed and that I'm now too old to conceive? Let me tell you, I'll bear another son much better than you – better still, to make you feel the insult more, I'll adopt one of my household slaves and give *him* those wings and torch, and bow and arrows too, and all that gear of mine, which I didn't give you to be used like this – for there was no allowance for this outfit from your father's estate. But you were badly brought up from a baby, quarrelsome, always insolently hitting your elders. Your own mother, me I say, you expose and abuse every day, battering me all the time, despising me, I suppose, as an unprotected female – and you're not afraid of that mighty warrior your stepfather. Naturally enough, seeing that you're in the habit of providing him with girls, to torment me with his infidelities. But I'll see to it that you're sorry for these games and find out that this marriage of yours has a sour and bitter taste. But now, being mocked like this, what am I to do? Where am I to turn? How am I to control this reptile? Shall I seek assistance from Sobriety, when I have so often offended her through this creature's wantonness? No, I won't, I won't, have any dealings with such an uncouth and unkempt female. But then the consolation of revenge isn't to be scorned, whatever its source. Her aid and hers alone is what I must enlist, to administer severe correction to this layabout, to undo his quiver, blunt his arrows, unstring his bow, put out his torch, and coerce him with some sharper corporal medicine. I'll believe that his insolence to me has been fully atoned for only when she has shaved off the locks to which I have so often imparted a golden sheen by my caressing hands, and cut off the wings which I have groomed with nectar from my own breasts.'

With these words she rushed violently out in a fury of truly Venerean anger. The first persons she met were Ceres and Juno, who seeing her face all swollen with rage, asked her why she was frowning so grimly and spoiling the shining beauty of her eyes. To which she answered: 'You've come just at the right moment to satisfy the desire with which my heart is burning. Please, I beg you, do your utmost to find that runaway fly-by-night Psyche for me, for you two must be well aware of the scandal of my house and of what my son – not that he deserves the name – has been doing.' They, knowing perfectly well what had happened, tried to soothe Venus' violent rage: 'Madam, what has your son done that's so dreadful that you are determined to thwart his pleasures and even want to destroy the one he loves? Is it really a crime, for heaven's sake, to have been so ready to give the glad eye to a nice girl? Don't you realize that he is a young man? You must have forgotten how old he is now. Perhaps because he carries his years so prettily, he always seems a boy to you? Are you, a mother and a woman of sense, to be forever inquiring into all his diversions, checking his little escapades, and showing up his love-affairs? Aren't you condemning in your fair son your own arts and pleasures? Gods and men alike will find it intolerable that you spread desire broadcast throughout the world, while you impose a bitter constraint on love in your own family and deny it admission to your own public academy of gallantry.' In this way, fearful of his arrows, did they flatter Cupid in his absence with their ingratiating defence of his cause. But Venus took it ill that her grievances should be treated so lightly, and cutting them short made off quickly in the other direction, back towards the sea.

Psyche meanwhile was wandering far and wide, searching day and night for her husband, and the sicker she was at heart, the more eager she was, if she could not mollify him by wifely endearments, at least to appease his anger by beseeching him as a slave. Seeing a temple on the top of a steep hill, 'Perhaps,' said she, 'my lord lives there'; at once she made for it, her pace, which had flagged in her unbroken fatigues, now quickened by hope and desire. Having stoutly climbed the lofty slopes she approached the shrine. There she saw ears of corn, some heaped up, some woven into garlands, together with ears of barley. There were also sickles and every kind of harvesting gear, all lying anyhow in neglect and confusion and looking, as happens in summer, as if they had just been dropped from the workers' hands. All these things Psyche carefully sorted and separated, each in its proper place, and arranged as they ought to be, thinking evidently that she should not neglect the shrines or worship of any god, but should implore the goodwill and pity of them all.

She was diligently and busily engaged on this task when bountiful Ceres found her, and with a deep sigh said: 'So, poor Psyche! There is Venus in her rage dogging your footsteps with painstaking inquiries through the whole world, singling you out for dire punishment, and demanding revenge with the whole power of her godhead; and here are you taking charge of my shrine and thinking of anything rather than your own safety.' Psyche fell down before her, and bedewing her feet with a flood of tears, her hair trailing on the ground, she implored the goddess's favour in an elaborate prayer: 'I beseech you, by this your fructifying hand, by the fertile rites of harvest, by the inviolate secrets of the caskets, by the winged chariot of your dragon-servants, by the furrows of the Sicilian fields, by the car that snatches and the earth that catches, by your daughter Proserpine's descent to her lightless wedding and her return to bright discovery, and all else that the sanctuary of Attic Eleusis conceals in silence: support the pitiful spirit of your suppliant Psyche. Allow me to hide for only a very few days among these heaps of corn, until the great goddess's fierce anger is soothed by the passing of time or at least until my strength is recruited from the fatigues of long suffering by an interval of rest.' Ceres answered: 'Your tearful prayers indeed move me and make me wish to help you; but I cannot offend my kinswoman, who is a dear friend of long standing and a thoroughly good sort. So you must leave this place at once, and think yourself lucky that you are not my prisoner.'

Disappointed and rebuffed, the prey of a double sadness, Psyche was retracing her steps, when in the half-light of a wooded valley which lay before her she saw a temple built with cunning art. Not wishing to neglect any prospect, however doubtful, of better hopes, but willing to implore the favour of any and every god, she drew near to the holy entrance. There she saw precious offerings and cloths lettered in gold affixed to trees and to the doorposts, attesting the name of the goddess to whom they were dedicated in gratitude for her aid. Then, kneeling and embracing the yet warm altar, she wiped away her tears and prayed: 'Sister and consort of great Jove, whether you are at home in your ancient shrine on Samos, which alone glories in having seen your birth, heard your first cries, and nourished your infancy; or whether you dwell in your rich abode in lofty Carthage, which worships you as a virgin riding the heavens on a lion; or whether by the banks of Inachus, who hails you now as bride of the Thunderer and queen of goddesses, you rule over the famous citadel of Argos; you who are worshipped by the whole East as Zygia and whom all the West calls Lucina: be in my desperate need Juno who Saves, and save me, worn out by the great sufferings I have gone through, from the danger that hangs over me. Have I not been told that it is you who are wont to come uncalled to the aid of pregnant women when they are in peril?' As she suppli-cated thus, Juno immediately manifested herself in all the awesome dignity of her godhead, and replied: 'Believe me, I should like to grant your prayers. But I cannot for shame oppose myself to the wishes of my daughter-in-law Venus, whom I have always loved as my own child. Then too I am prevented by the laws which forbid me to receive another person's runaway slaves against their master's wishes.'

Psyche was completely disheartened by this second shipwreck that Fortune had contrived for her, and with no prospect of finding her winged husband she gave up all hope of salvation. So she took counsel with herself: 'Now what other aid can I try, or bring to bear on my distresses, seeing that not even the goddesses' influence can help me, though they would like to? Trapped in this net, where can I turn? What shelter is there, what dark hiding-place, where I can escape the unavoidable eyes of great Venus? No, this is the end: I must summon up a man's spirit, boldly renounce my empty remnants of hope, give myself up to my mistress of my own free will, and appease her violence by submission, late though it will be. And perhaps he whom I have sought so long may be found there in his mother's house.' So, prepared for submission with all its dangers, indeed for certain destruction, she thought over how she should begin the prayer she would utter.

Venus, however, had given up earthbound expedients in her search, and set off for heaven. She ordered to be prepared the car that Vulcan the goldsmith god had lovingly perfected with cunning workmanship and given her as a betrothal present – a work of art that made its impression by what his refining tools had pared away, valuable through the very loss of gold. Of the many doves quartered round their mistress's chamber there came forth four all white; stepping joyfully and twisting their coloured necks around they submitted to the jewelled yoke, then with their mistress on board they gaily took the air. The car was attended by a retinue of sportive sparrows frolicking around with their noisy chatter, and of other sweet-voiced birds who, singing in honey-toned strains, harmoniously proclaimed the advent of the goddess. The clouds parted, heaven opened for his daughter, and highest Aether joyfully welcomed the goddess; great Venus' tuneful entourage has no fear of ambushes from eagles or rapacious hawks.

She immediately headed for Jove's royal citadel and haughtily demanded an essential loan – the services of Mercury, the loud-voiced god. Jove nodded his dark brow, and she in triumph left heaven then and there with Mercury, to whom she earnestly spoke: 'Arcadian brother, you know well that your sister Venus has never done anything without Mercury's assistance, and you must be aware too of how long it is that I have been trying in vain to find my skulking handmaid. All we can do now is for you as herald to make public proclamation of a reward for her discovery. Do my bidding then at once, and describe clearly the signs by which she can be recognized, so that if anybody is charged with illegally concealing her, he cannot defend himself with a plea of ignorance'; and with these words she gave him a paper with Psyche's name and the other details. That done, she returned straight home.

Mercury duly obeyed her. Passing far and wide among the peoples he carried out his assignment and made proclamation as ordered: 'If any man can recapture or show the hiding-place of a king's runaway daughter, the slave of Venus, by name Psyche, let him report to Mercury the crier behind the South turning-point of the

Circus, and by way of reward for his information he shall receive from Venus herself seven sweet kisses and an extra one deeply honeyed with the sweetness of her thrusting tongue.' This proclamation of Mercury's and the desire for such a reward aroused eager competition all over the world. Its effect on Psyche was to put an end to all her hesitation. As she neared her mistress's door she was met by one of Venus' household named Habit, who on seeing her cried out at the top of her voice: 'At last, you worthless slut, you've begun to realize you have a mistress? Or will you with your usual impudence pretend you don't know how much trouble we've had looking for you? A good thing you've fallen into *my* hands; you're held in the grip of Orcus, and you can be sure you won't have to wait long for the punishment of your disobedience.' So saying, she laid violent hands on Psyche's hair and dragged her inside unresisting. As soon as Venus saw her brought in and presented to her, she laughed shrilly, as people do in a rage; and shaking her head and scratching her right ear, 'So,' she said, 'you have finally condescended to pay your respects to your mother-in-law? Or is it your husband you've come to visit, who lies under threat of death from the wound you've dealt him? But don't worry, I will receive you as a good daughter-in-law deserves.' Then, 'Where are my handmaids Care and Sorrow?' she asked. They were called in, and Psyche was handed over to them to be tormented. In obedience to their mistress's orders they whipped the wretched girl and afflicted her with every other kind of torture, and then brought her back to face the goddess. Venus, laughing again, exclaimed: 'Look at her, trying to arouse my pity through the allurement of her swollen belly, whose glorious offspring is to make me, thank you very much, a happy grandmother. What joy, to be called grandmother in the flower of my age and to hear the son of a vile slave styled Venus' grandson! But why am I talking about sons? This isn't a marriage between equals, and what's more it took place in the country, without witnesses, and without his father's consent, and can't be held to be legitimate. So it will be born a bastard, if indeed I allow you to bear it at all.'

With these words, she flew at Psyche, ripped her clothes to shreds, tore her hair, boxed her ears, and beat her unmercifully. Then she took wheat and barley and millet and poppy-seed and chick-peas and lentils and beans, mixed them thoroughly all together in a single heap, and told Psyche: 'Now, since it seems to me that, ugly slave that you are, you can earn the favours of your lovers only by diligent drudgery, I'm now going to put your merit to the test myself. Sort out this random heap of seeds, and let me see the work completed this evening, with each kind of grain properly arranged and separated.' And leaving her with the enormous heap of grains, Venus went off to a wedding-dinner. Psyche did not attempt to touch the disordered and unmanageable mass, but stood in silent stupefaction, stunned by this monstrous command. Then there appeared an ant, one of those miniature farmers; grasping the size of the problem, pitying the plight of the great god's bedfellow and execrating her mother-in-law's cruelty, it rushed round eagerly to summon and convene the whole assembly of the local ants. 'Have pity,' it cried, 'nimble children of Earth the all-mother, have pity and run with all speed to the aid of the sweet girl-wife of Love in her peril.' In wave after wave the six-footed tribes poured in to the rescue, and working at top speed they sorted out the whole heap grain by grain, separated and distributed the seed by kinds, and vanished swiftly from view.

At nightfall Venus returned from the banquet flushed with wine, fragrant with perfume, and garlanded all over with brilliant roses. When she saw the wonderful exactness with which the task had been performed, 'Worthless wretch!' she exclaimed, 'this is not your doing or the work of your hands, but his whose fancy you have taken – so much the worse indeed for you, and for him'; and throwing Psyche a crust of coarse bread she took herself to bed. Meanwhile Cupid was under strict guard, in solitary confinement in one room at the back of the palace, partly to stop him from aggravating his wound through his impetuous passion, partly to stop him from seeing his beloved. So then the two lovers, though under the same roof, were kept apart and endured a melancholy night. As soon as Dawn took horse, Venus called Psyche and said: 'You see that wood which stretches along the banks of the river which washes it in passing, and the bushes at its edge which look down on the nearby spring? Sheep that shine with fleece of real gold wander and graze there unguarded. Of that precious wool see that you get a tuft by hook or by crook and bring it to me directly.'

Psyche set out willingly, not because she expected to fulfil her task, but meaning to find a respite from her sufferings by throwing herself from a rock into the river.

But then from the river a green reed, source of sweet music, divinely inspired by the gentle whisper of the soft breeze, thus prophesied: 'Psyche, tried by much suffering, do not pollute my holy waters by your pitiable death. This is not the moment to approach these fearsome sheep, while they are taking in heat from the blazing sun and are maddened by fierce rage; their horns are sharp and their foreheads hard as stone, and they often attack and kill men with their poisonous bites. Rather, until the midday heat of the sun abates and the flock is quietened by the soothing breeze off the river, you can hide under that tall plane which drinks the current together with me. Then, when their rage is calmed and their attention is relaxed, shake the branches of the nearby trees, and you will find the golden wool which sticks everywhere in their entwined stems.'

So this open-hearted reed in its humanity showed the unfortunate Psyche the way to safety. She paid due heed to its salutary advice and acted accordingly: she did everything she was told and had no trouble in helping herself to a heaped-up armful of the golden softness to bring back to Venus. Not that, from her mistress at least, the successful outcome of her second trial earned her any approval. Venus bent her brows and with an acid smile said: 'I am not deceived: this exploit too is that lecher's. Now, however, I shall really exert myself to find out whether you have a truly stout heart and a good head on your shoulders. You see the top of the steep mountain that looms over that lofty crag, from which there flows down the dark waters of a black spring, to be received in a basin of the neighbouring valley, and then to water the marshes of Styx and feed the hoarse streams of Cocytus? There, just where the spring gushes out on the very summit, draw off its ice-cold water and bring it to me instantly in this jar.' So saying she gave her an urn hollowed out from crystal, adding yet direr threats.

Psyche eagerly quickened her pace towards the mountain-top, expecting to find at least an end of her wretched existence there. But as soon as she approached the summit that Venus had shown her, she saw the deadly difficulty of her enormous task. There stood a rock, huge and lofty, too rough and treacherous to climb; from jaws of stone in its midst it poured out its grim stream, which first gushed from a sloping cleft, then plunged steeply to be hidden in the narrow channel of the path it had carved out for itself, and so to fall by secret ways into the neighbouring valley. To left and right she saw emerging from the rocky hollows fierce serpents with long necks outstretched, their eyes enslaved to unwinking vigilance, forever on the watch and incessantly wakeful. And now the very water defended itself in speech, crying out repeatedly 'Be off!' and 'What are you doing? Look out!' and 'What are you about? Take care!' and 'Fly!' and 'You'll die!' Psyche was turned to stone by the sheer impossibility of her task, and though her body was present her senses left her: overwhelmed completely by the weight of dangers she was powerless to cope with, she could not even weep, the last consolation.

But the suffering of this innocent soul did not escape the august eyes of Providence. For the regal bird of almighty Jove, the ravisher eagle, suddenly appeared with outspread wings, and remembering his former service, how prompted by Cupid he had stolen the Phrygian cupbearer for Jupiter, brought timely aid. In honour of the god's power, and seeing his wife's distress, he left Jove's pathways in the heights, and gliding down before the girl he addressed her: 'Do you, naive as you are and inexperienced in such things, hope to be able to steal a single drop of this most holy and no less terrible spring, or even touch it? You must have heard that this water of Styx is feared by the gods themselves, even Jupiter, and that the oaths which mortals swear by the power of the gods, the gods swear by the majesty of Styx. Give me that urn' – and seizing and holding it he took off, and poising himself on his mighty hovering wings he steered to left and right between the raging jaws and flickering three-forked tongues of the dragons, to draw off the waters, though they resisted and warned him to retreat while he could do so in safety – he pretending meanwhile that he had been ordered to fetch it by Venus and that he was in her service; and thus it was a little easier for him to approach.

Psyche joyfully received the full urn and took it back at once to Venus. Even then, however, she could not satisfy the wishes of the cruel goddess. Threatening her with yet worse outrages, she addressed Psyche with a deadly smile: 'I really think you must be some sort of great and profoundly accomplished witch to have carried out so promptly orders like these of mine. But you still have to do me this service, my dear. Take this casket' (giving it to her) 'and be off with you to the Underworld and the ghostly abode of Orcus himself. Present it to

Proserpine and say: "Venus begs that you send her a little of your beauty, enough at least for one short day. For the supply that she had, she has quite used up and exhausted in looking after her ailing son." Come back in good time, for I must make myself up from it before going to the theatre of the gods.'

Then indeed Psyche knew that her last hour had come and that all disguise was at an end, and that she was being openly sent to instant destruction. So much was clear, seeing that she was being made to go on her own two feet to Tartarus and the shades. Without delay she made for a certain lofty tower, meaning to throw herself off it: for in that way she thought she could most directly and economically go down to the Underworld. But the tower suddenly broke into speech: 'Why, poor child, do you want to destroy yourself by a death-leap? Why needlessly give up at this last ordeal? Once your soul is separated from your body, then indeed you will go straight to the pit of Tartarus, but there will be no coming back for you. Listen to me. Not far from here is Sparta, a famous city of Greece. Near to it, hidden in a trackless countryside, you must find Taenarus. There you'll see the breathing-hole of Dis, and through its gaping portals the forbidden road; once you have passed the threshold and entrusted yourself to it, you will fare by a direct track to the very palace of Orcus. But you must not go through that darkness empty-handed as you are; you must carry in your hands cakes of barley meal soaked in wine and honey, and in your mouth two coins. When you have gone a good way along the infernal road you will meet a lame donkey loaded with wood and

with a lame driver; he will ask you to hand him some
sticks fallen from the load, but you must say nothing and
pass by in silence. Directly after that you will come to
the river of death. Its harbourmaster is Charon, who
ferries wayfarers to the other bank in his boat of skins
only on payment of the fee which he immediately
demands. So it seems that avarice lives even among the
dead, and a great god like Charon, Dis's Collector, does
nothing for nothing. A poor man on his deathbed must
make sure of his journey-money, and if he hasn't got the
coppers to hand, he won't be allowed to expire. To this
unkempt old man you must give one of your coins as
his fare, making him take it himself from your mouth.
Then, while you are crossing the sluggish stream, an old
dead man swimming over will raise his decaying hands
to ask you to haul him aboard; but you must not be
swayed by pity, which is forbidden to you. When you
are across and have gone a little way, some old women
weavers will ask you to lend a hand for a moment to set
up their loom; but here too you must not become
involved. For all these and many other ruses will be
inspired by Venus to make you drop one of your cakes.
Don't think the loss of a paltry barley cake a light thing:
if you lose one you will thereby lose the light of the sun.
For a huge dog with three enormous heads, a monstrous
and fearsome brute, barking thunderously and with
empty menace at the dead, whom he can no longer
harm, is on perpetual guard before the threshold and
dark halls of Proserpine, and watches over the empty
house of Dis. Him you can muzzle by letting him have
one of your cakes; passing him easily by you will come

directly to Proserpine, who will receive you kindly and courteously, urging you to take a soft seat and join her in a rich repast. But you must sit on the ground and ask for some coarse bread; when you have eaten it you can tell her why you have come, and then taking what you are given you can return. Buy off the fierce dog with your other cake, and then giving the greedy ferryman the coin you have kept, you will cross the river and retrace your earlier path until you regain the light of heaven above. But this prohibition above all I bid you observe: do not open or look into the box that you bear or pry at all into its hidden store of divine beauty.'

So this far-sighted tower accomplished its prophetic task. Psyche without delay made for Taenarus, where she duly equipped herself with coins and cakes and made the descent to the Underworld. Passing in silence the lame donkey-driver, paying her fare to the ferryman, ignoring the plea of the dead swimmer, rejecting the crafty entreaties of the weavers, and appeasing the fearsome rage of the dog with her cake, she arrived at Proserpine's palace. She declined her hostess's offer of a soft seat and rich food, and sitting on the ground before her feet, content with a piece of coarse bread, she reported Venus' commission. The box was immediately taken away to be filled and closed up in private, and given back to Psyche. By the device of the second cake she muzzled the dog's barking, and giving the ferryman her second coin she returned from the Underworld much more briskly than she had come. Having regained and worshipped the bright light of day, though in a hurry to complete her mission, she madly succumbed to her reckless curiosity. 'What a fool I am,' said she, 'to be carrying divine beauty and not to help myself even to a tiny bit of it, so as perhaps to please my beautiful lover.' So saying she opened the box. But she found nothing whatever in it, no beauty, but only an infernal sleep, a sleep truly Stygian, which when the lid was taken off and it was let out at once took possession of her and diffused itself in a black cloud of oblivion throughout her whole body, so that overcome by it she collapsed on the spot where she stood in the pathway, and lay motionless, a mere sleeping corpse.

But Cupid's wound had now healed and, his strength returned, he could no longer bear to be parted for so long from Psyche. He escaped from the high window of the room in which he was confined; and, with his wings restored by his long rest, he flew off at great speed to the side of his Psyche. Carefully wiping off the sleep and replacing it where it had been in the box, he roused her with a harmless prick from one of his arrows. 'There, poor wretch,' he said, 'you see how yet again curiosity has been your undoing. But meanwhile you must complete the mission assigned you by my mother with all diligence; the rest I will see to.' So saying, her lover nimbly took flight, while Psyche quickly took back Proserpine's gift to Venus.

Meanwhile Cupid, eaten up with love, looking ill, and dreading his mother's new-found austerity, became himself again. On swift wings he made his way to the very summit of heaven and pleaded his cause as a suppliant with great Jupiter. Jupiter took Cupid's face in his hand, pulled it to his own, and kissed him, saying: 'In spite of the fact, dear boy, that you have never paid me the respect decreed me by the gods in council, but have constantly shot and wounded this breast of mine by which the behaviour of the elements and the movements of the heavenly bodies are regulated, defiling it repeatedly with lustful adventures on earth, compromising my reputation and character by low intrigues in defiance of the laws, the Lex Julia included, and of public morals, changing my majestic features into the base shapes of snakes, of fire, of wild animals, of birds and of farmyard beasts – yet in spite of all, remembering my clemency and that you grew up in my care, I will do what you ask. But you must take care to guard against your rivals; and if there is now any pre-eminently lovely girl on earth, you are bound to pay me back with her for this good turn.'

So saying, he ordered Mercury to summon all the gods immediately to assembly, proclaiming that any absentees from this heavenly meeting would be liable to a fine of ten thousand sesterces. This threat at once filled the divine theatre; and Jupiter, towering on his lofty throne, announced his decision. 'Conscript deities enrolled in the register of the Muses, you undoubtedly know this young man well, and how I have reared him with my own hands. I have decided that the hot-blooded impulses of his first youth must somehow be bridled; his name has been besmirched long enough in common report by adultery and all kinds of licentious behaviour. We must take away all opportunity for this and confine his youthful excess in the bonds of marriage. He has chosen a girl and had her virginity: let him have and hold her, and embracing Psyche for ever enjoy his beloved.' Then turning to Venus, 'Daughter,' he said, 'do not be downcast or fear for your great lineage or social standing because of this marriage with a mortal. I shall arrange for it to be not unequal but legitimate and in accordance with the civil law.' Then he ordered Psyche to be brought by Mercury and introduced into heaven. Handing her a cup of ambrosia, 'Take this, Psyche,' he said, 'and be immortal. Never shall Cupid quit the tie that binds you, but this marriage shall be perpetual for you both.'

No sooner said than done: a lavish wedding-feast appeared. In the place of honour reclined Psyche's husband, with his wife in his arms, and likewise Jupiter with his Juno, and then the other gods in order of precedence. Cups of nectar were served to Jove by his own cupbearer, the shepherd lad, and to the others by Liber; Vulcan cooked the dinner; the Seasons made everything colourful with roses and other flowers; the Graces sprinkled perfumes; the Muses discoursed tuneful music. Then Apollo sang to the lyre, and Venus, fitting her steps to the sweet music, danced in all her beauty, having arranged a production in which the Muses were chorus and played the tibia, while a Satyr and a little Pan sang to the shepherd's pipe.

Thus was Psyche married to Cupid with all proper ceremony, and when her time came there was born to them a daughter, whom we call Pleasure.

Book I

*Prologue in which the author introduces himself – Lucius
follows suit – on the way to Thessaly – Aristomenes'
story – arrival at Hypata and reception by Milo – a
puzzling experience in the market – hungry to bed*

Now, what I propose in this Milesian* discourse is to
string together for you a series of different stories and to
charm your ears, kind reader, with amusing gossip –
always assuming that you are not too proud to look at
an Egyptian book written with the sharpness of a pen
from the Nile; and to make you marvel at a story of men's
shapes and fortunes changed into other forms and then
restored all over again. So I'll begin. But who is this? In
brief: Attic Hymettus, the Isthmus of Corinth, and Spar-
tan Taenarus, fruitful lands immortalized in yet more
fruitful books, these make up my ancient ancestry. It
was there that I served my earliest apprenticeship to the
language of Athens. Later, arriving in Rome a stranger to
its culture, with no teacher to show me the way, by my
own painful efforts I attacked and mastered the Latin
language. That then is my excuse, if as an unpractised
speaker of the foreign idiom of the Roman courts I should
stumble and give offence. In fact this linguistic metamor-
phosis suits the style of writing I have tackled here – the

* In the style of Aristides of Miletus, i.e. popular and informal.

trick, you might call it, of changing literary horses at the gallop. It is a Grecian story that I am going to begin. Give me your ear, reader: you will enjoy yourself.

I was on my way to Thessaly – for on my mother's side our family goes back there, being proud to number among our ancestors the distinguished philosopher Plutarch and his nephew Sextus – I was on my way, I say, to Thessaly on particular business. I had negotiated a succession of steep passes, muddy valleys, dewy pastures, and sticky ploughlands, and like me, my horse, who was native-bred, a pure white animal, was getting pretty tired. Thinking I might shake off my own saddle-weariness by a little exercise, I dismounted, wiped my horse down, rubbed his forehead scientifically, caressed his ears, and took off his bridle; then I led him on at a gentle pace, to let him get rid of his fatigue through the natural restorative of a snack. And so, while he, with his head turned to the verges as he passed, was taking his breakfast on the hoof, I caught up with two fellow wayfarers who happened to have gone on a short way ahead. As I began to eavesdrop, one was roaring with laughter and saying: 'Do give over lying like that – I've never heard anything so utterly absurd.'

At that I, thirsting as always for novelty, struck in: 'No, please,' I said, 'let me in on this – not that I'm nosy, it's just that I'm the sort of person who likes to know everything, or at least as much as I can. And an agreeable and amusing yarn or two will lessen the steepness of this hill we're climbing.' 'Yes,' said the first speaker, 'these lies are just as true as it would be to say that because of magic rivers can suddenly reverse their flow, the sea be becalmed, the winds cease to blow, the sun stand still, the moon be milked of her dew, the stars uprooted, the daylight banished, the night prolonged.' Then I, emboldened, said: 'You, sir, who began this story, please don't be annoyed or too disgusted to tell us the rest'; and to the other man, 'But what you are stupidly refusing to listen to and stubbornly pooh-poohing may very well be a true report. Really, I think you are being ignorant and perverse when you account as a lie anything you've never heard of or aren't familiar with the sight of or just find too difficult for your understanding to grasp. If you look into these things a little more closely, you'll find out that they aren't only reliably attested but can easily happen. Look at me, yesterday evening: trying desperately to keep my end up at dinner, I rashly tried to cram down a piece of cheesecake that was too big, and the gooey stuff lodged in my throat and blocked my windpipe – I was very nearly a goner. Then again, when I was in Athens only the other day, in front of the Painted Porch, I saw with these two eyes a juggler swallow a sharp cavalry sabre, point first; and then the same man, encouraged by a small donation, lowered a hunting spear right down into his inside, lethal point first. And then, lo and behold, above the blade of the lance, where the shaft of the inverted weapon entered the man's throat and stood up over his head, there appeared a boy, pretty as a girl, who proceeded to wreathe himself round it in a bonelessly sensuous dance. We were all lost in amazement; you'd have thought it was Aesculapius' own rough-hewn staff, with his sacred serpent twining sinuously round it. But sir, please do go on with your story. I promise you I'll believe it even if our friend here won't, and at the first inn we come to I'll stand you lunch – there's your payment secured.'

'Very kind of you,' he said, 'but I'll start my story again in any case, thanks all the same. First however let me swear to you by this all-seeing divine Sun that what I'm going to tell you really happened; and if you get to the next town in Thessaly, you'll be left in no doubt; all this was done in public and everyone there is still talking about it. But to let you know who I am, and where I come from: my name is Aristomenes, from Aegium. Let me tell you how I get a living: I travel all over Thessaly and Aetolia and Boeotia in honey and cheese and suchlike innkeeper's staples. So, hearing that at Hypata – it's the most important place in Thessaly – there was some new and particularly tasty cheese on offer at a very reasonable price, I hurried off there to put in a bid for the lot. But as tends to happen, I got off on the wrong foot and was disappointed in my hope of making a killing: a wholesaler called Lupus had bought it all the day before.

'So, worn out by my useless hurry, I took myself off at sundown to the public baths; and who should I see there but my old friend Socrates. He was sitting on the ground, half wrapped in a tattered old coat, his face sickly yellow so that I hardly recognized him, miserably thin, looking just like one of those bits of Fortune's flotsam one sees begging in the streets. Seeing him looking like this, though as I say I knew him extremely well, it was with some hesitation that I went up to him. "Socrates, my dear fellow," I said, "what's up? Why are you looking like this? What have they done to you? Back home you've been mourned and given up for dead; and your children have been assigned guardians by the court. Your wife has given you a formal funeral; and now, disfigured by months of grieving and having wept herself nearly blind, she's being urged by her parents to cheer up the family misfortunes by getting happily married again. And here are you, looking like a ghost and putting us all to shame."

'"Aristomenes," he said, "you just don't understand the deceitful twists and turns of Fortune, her surprise attacks, her reversals of direction," and as he spoke he covered his face, which had become red with shame, with his rags and patches, leaving himself naked from navel to groin. I couldn't bear the pitiful sight of his distress, and tried to pull him to his feet. But he, keeping his head covered, cried: "Leave me alone, leave me, and let Fortune go on enjoying the spectacle of this trophy that she's set up." However, I got him to come with me, and taking off one of my tunics I dressed or at least covered him up with it, and took him off to the baths. I got him oil and towels and with much effort scrubbed off the horrible filth he was encrusted with; and then when he had been thoroughly put to rights (by which time I was worn out myself and was hard put to it to hold him up), I took him back to my inn, put him to bed to recover, gave him a good dinner and a relaxing glass or two of wine, and chatted to him to calm him down.

'He was just beginning to talk freely, to crack the odd joke, even to get mildly flippant and answer back, when suddenly, heaving an excruciating sigh from the depths of his chest and passionately slapping his forehead, he broke out: "Gods, what miserable luck! It was only because I went in search of a bit of pleasure, to see a gladiatorial show I'd heard a lot about, that I got into this dreadful mess. As you know, I'd gone to Macedonia on business. I'd been hard at it there for nine months, and having made a decent profit I was on my way home. Not far from Larissa, where I was planning to see the show on my way through, I was waylaid in a wild and watery glen by a gang of bandits – absolute monsters – and robbed of everything I had, though in the end I escaped with my life. Reduced to this desperate state, I took shelter at an inn kept by a woman called Meroe, not at all bad-looking for her age. I told her everything, why I'd been away so long, my anxiety to get home, and the lamentable story of the robbery. She welcomed me more than kindly, treating me first to a good dinner, free gratis and for nothing, and then to a share of her bed – she really was on heat. And that's how I came to grief: that first night with her was the start of a long and degrading association. Even the rags which the robbers had generously left me to cover myself with, even those I made over to her, along with the pittance I earned as a porter while I was still fit enough for the work. And that's how this worthy wife, so called, and the malevolence of Fortune between them have reduced me to what you saw just now."

'"Well, damn it," I said, "you deserve anything you get and worse than that, for preferring the pleasure of fornicating with a leathery old hag to your home and children." But he put his finger to his lips and looked utterly horrified. "Shh, quiet," he said, looking round to see that we weren't overheard. "Don't talk like that about a woman with superhuman powers, or your rash tongue will get you into trouble." "Really?" I said. "What sort of woman is this mighty tavern-queen?" "A witch," he answered, "with supernatural powers; she can bring down the sky, raise up the earth, solidify springs, dissolve mountains, raise the dead, send the gods down below, blot out the stars, and illuminate Hell itself." "Come on," I said, "spare me the histrionics and let's have it in plain language." "Well," he said, "do you want to hear one or two of her exploits? There are lots I could tell you about. It's not only our own people that she can make fall madly in love with her, but the Indians, the Ethiopians – both lots – even the Antipodeans; that's nothing, the merest ABC of her art. But let me tell you what she did in full view of a crowd of eyewitnesses.

'"When one of her lovers was unfaithful to her, with a single word she turned him into a beaver, because when they're afraid of being caught beavers escape their pursuers by biting off their balls – the idea being that something like that would happen to him. An innkeeper, who was a neighbour and therefore a trade rival, she changed into frog; and now the poor old chap swims around in a barrel of his own wine and greets his old customers with a polite croak as he squats there in the lees. Another time she changed a lawyer who appeared against her in court into a ram, and it's as a ram that he now pleads his cases. Again, the wife of another of her lovers she condemned to perpetual pregnancy for being witty at her expense; she shut up the woman's womb and halted the growth of the foetus, so that it's now eight years (we've all done the sum) that this unfortunate creature has been swollen with her burden, as if it was an elephant that she was going to produce.

'"This sort of thing kept happening, and a lot of people suffered at her hands, so that public indignation grew and spread; and a meeting was held at which it was decided that on the following day she should receive drastic punishment by stoning to death. However, she thwarted this move by the strength of her spells – just like the famous Medea when, having obtained a single day's grace from Creon, she used it to burn up the old king's palace, his daughter, and himself, with the crown of fire. Just so Meroe sacrificed into a trench to the powers of darkness (she told me all this the other day when she was drunk), and shut up the whole population in their houses by silent supernatural force. For two whole days they couldn't undo their bolts or get their doors open or even break through their walls, until in the end they came to an agreement among themselves and all called out, swearing by what they held most sacred, that they would not lay a finger on her and that if anybody had other ideas they would come to her assistance. So she was appeased and let them all off, except for the man who had convened the public meeting. Him she whisked off at dead of night, with his whole house – walls, foundations, the ground it stood on – still shut up, a hundred miles away to another town which was situated on the top of a rocky and waterless mountain. And since the houses there were too closely packed to allow room for another one, she simply dumped it outside the town gates and decamped."

' "My dear Socrates," I said, "what you tell me is as ghastly as it's astonishing. You really have made me very uneasy – no, you've terrified me. It's not just a pinprick of anxiety but a positive spearthrust that you've inflicted – the fear that the old woman may invoke some supernatural aid as she's done before to eavesdrop on this conversation. So let's get to bed straight away, and when we've slept off our fatigue let's get as far as possible away from here before it's light." Before I had finished offering this advice, my friend, who had been tried to the limit by so many wearing experiences and more wine than he was used to, was fast asleep and snoring noisily. So I closed the door and shot the bolts firmly, and also wedged my bed hard up against the hinges and lay down on it. At first my fear kept me awake for a time, but then about midnight I dropped off. Hardly had I done so when suddenly (you wouldn't think a whole gang of robbers could manage such an onslaught) the door was thrown open, or rather broken down and torn right off its hinges and sent crashing to the ground. My bed, which was only a cot, with a foot missing and riddled with worm, was overturned by this violent shock, and I was hurled out of it and rolled on to the floor with the bed upside down on top of me and hiding me.

'Then I discovered that some emotions naturally express themselves by their opposites. Just as one very often weeps tears of joy, so then, utterly terrified as I was, I couldn't help laughing at the idea of myself as a tortoise. Grovelling there in the dirt I was able from under the protection of my resourceful bed to get a sideways view of what was happening. I saw two elderly women, one carrying a lighted lamp, the other a sponge and a naked sword. So arrayed, they stood on either side of Socrates, who was still sound asleep. The one with the sword spoke first: "There he is, sister Panthia, my beloved Endymion, my Ganymede, who by night and day has played fast and loose with my tender youth, who scorns my love, and not content with calumniating me is trying to escape me. I take it I'm supposed to play abandoned Calypso to his wily Ulysses, left to mourn in perpetual solitude?" And then she pointed and indicated me to Panthia: "But here we have our friend Aristomenes the Counsellor, who is the author of this escape plan and now lies on the ground under that bed within a hair's-breadth of death, watching all this and thinking that the injuries he has done me will go unpunished. One day – what am I saying, now, this very moment – I'll make him sorry for his past impudence and his present curiosity."

'Hearing this I was in agony, drenched in an icy sweat and shaking all over, so that the bed too was convulsed by my shudders and heaved up and down on top of me. Then said the amiable Panthia: "Now, sister, shall we take this one first and tear him limb from limb like Bacchantes, or tie him down and castrate him?" But Meroe – for she it was, as I realized from what Socrates had told me – said: "No, let him survive to give a modest burial to the body of his poor friend," and twisting Socrates' head to one side she buried her sword up to the hilt in the left-hand side of his throat, catching the blood that spurted out in a leather bottle so neatly that not a drop was spilled. This I saw with my own eyes.

Next dear Meroe, wanting I suppose to keep as closely as possible to the sacrificial forms, plunged her hand into the wound right down to his entrails, rummaged about, and pulled out my poor friend's heart. At this he let out through the wound in his throat, which the violent stroke of the sword had totally severed, an inarticulate whistling sound, and gave up the ghost. Then Panthia, blocking the gaping wound with her sponge, "Now, sponge," she said, "you were born in the sea – take care not to cross a river." With these words they left, but first they pulled the bed off me and squatted down and emptied their bladders over my face, leaving me soaked in their filthy piss.

'The moment they had gone the door reverted to normal: the hinges flew back into position, the bars returned to the doorposts, and the bolts shot back into the slot. As for me, I remained where I was, grovelling on the floor, fainting, naked, cold and drenched in piss, just like a new-born child – or rather half dead, a post-humous survivor of myself, an absolutely certain candidate for crucifixion. "What's going to happen to me," I said to myself, "when he's found in the morning with his throat cut? I can tell the truth, but who'll believe me? I can hear them now. 'Couldn't you at least have called for help if you couldn't cope with a woman – a big chap like you? A man murdered before your eyes, and not a peep out of you? And how is it that you weren't likewise made away with by these female desperadoes? Why should their cruelty have spared a witness who could inform against them? So, you escaped Death; now go back to him!' "

'While I was going over this in my mind again and again, the night wore on. The best plan then seemed to be to get clear surreptitiously before dawn and to take the road, though I had no very clear idea where to go. So I shouldered my luggage and tried to undo the bolts; but the upright and conscientious door, which earlier had unbarred itself so readily, now only opened with much reluctance and after many turnings of the key. Then, "Hey, porter," I called, "where are you? Open the front door. I want to be off early." The porter was lying on the ground behind the door and was still half-asleep. "Have some sense," he said. "Don't you know the roads are stiff with robbers, and you want to start out at this time of night? You may have some crime on your conscience that makes you eager to die, but I'm not such a fathead as to want to take your place." "It's nearly light," I said, "and anyway, what can robbers take away from a traveller who's got nothing? Don't be stupid: you know that ten wrestlers can't strip a naked man." But he, drowsy and half-asleep, turned over in bed and muttered: "Anyway, how do I know you haven't murdered your companion that you came in with last night and aren't trying to save yourself by doing a bunk?"

'At that moment, I remember, I saw the earth opening and the depths of Hell, and Cerberus hungering for me; and I realized that it wasn't in pity that dear old Meroe had spared my life, but in a spirit of sadism, saving me for the cross. So I went back to my room to mull over the form my suicide was to take. Since the only lethal weapon provided by Fortune was my bed, "Now, now, O bed," I cried, "my dearest bed, thou who hast endured

with me so many sufferings, confidant and beholder of
the night's happenings, the only witness to my innocence
that I can call against my accusers, do you provide me
as I hasten to the shades with the weapon that shall save
me." With these words I set about undoing the cord
with which it was strung and made one end of it fast to
a beam which jutted out under the window; the other
end I knotted firmly into a noose, and then climbing on
the bed and mounting to my doom I put my head into the
halter. But when I kicked the support away, so that the
rope, tightened round my throat by my weight, should
cut off the function of my breathing – at that moment
the rotten old rope broke, and I fell from where I was
standing on to Socrates, who lay nearby, and rolled with
him on to the floor. And precisely at that very same
moment the porter burst abruptly in, shouting: "Where
are you? You wanted to be off at dead of night, and now
you're back in bed and snoring!" At this, aroused either
by my fall or the porter's raucous bellowing, Socrates
was on his feet first, remarking: "No wonder travellers
hate all innkeepers! Look at this officious oaf, shoving
in where he's not wanted – to see what he can steal,
I expect – and waking me up with his noise when I was
fast asleep and still tired out."

'I then got up too, happily revived by this unexpected
stroke of luck. "There, O most faithful of porters," I said,
"you see my companion and brother, the one that last
night, when you were drunk, you accused me of mur-
dering"; and as I spoke I embraced Socrates and kissed
him. He was shocked by the smell of the foul fluid with
which the witches had drenched me, and pushed me

violently away, shouting "Get off me, you stink like the worst kind of urinal", and then proceeded to ask me facetiously why I smelled like that. Embarrassed and on the spur of the moment I cracked some stupid joke to divert his attention to another subject. Then, slapping him on the back, I said: "Come on, let's be off and enjoy an early start." So, shouldering my traps, I paid the bill, and we set out.

'When we had gone some way the sun rose; and now that it was fully light, I looked very closely at my friend's neck where I had seen the sword go in, and I said to myself: "You're crazy; you were dead drunk and had a horrible dream. There's Socrates whole, sound and unharmed. Where's the wound? Where's the sponge? And where's the fresh deep scar?" Aloud I said: "The doctors are quite right when they tell us that eating and drinking too much causes nightmares. Look at me; I had a drop too much yesterday evening, and I passed a night of such dreadful threatening dreams that I still can't believe I'm not spattered and defiled with human gore." He smiled and said: "It's not blood but piss you were drenched with. But to tell the truth, I too had a dream, that my throat was cut; I had a pain there, and I thought the heart was plucked out of me – and even now I feel faint, my knees are trembling and I can't walk properly. I think I need something to eat to put the life back in me." "Right," I answered, "I've got some breakfast all ready for you," and taking off my knapsack I quickly gave him some bread and cheese, adding, "let's sit down under that plane tree."

'This we did, and I too had a little something. He was

eating greedily, but as I watched him, I saw that his face was becoming drawn and waxy pale, and his strength seemed to be ebbing away. Indeed he was so altered by this deathly change of complexion that I panicked, thinking of those Furies of last night; and the first piece of bread I'd taken, not a very big one, lodged right in my throat and refused either to go down or to come back up. What increased my alarm was that there was almost nobody about. Who was going to believe that one of a pair of companions had been done in without foul play on the part of the other? Meanwhile Socrates, having made short work of the food, became desperately thirsty, as well he might, having wolfed down the best part of a first-rate cheese. Not far from the plane tree there flowed a gentle stream, its current so slow that it looked like a placid pool, all silver and glass. "There," I said, "quench your thirst in that limpid spring." He got up, and finding a place that sloped down to the water, he knelt and leaned over eagerly to drink. He had hardly touched the surface with his lips when the wound in his throat gaped wide open to the bottom and the sponge shot out, followed by a little blood. His lifeless body nearly pitched headlong into the water, but I managed to get hold of one foot and drag him laboriously up the bank. There, after mourning him as best I could in the circumstances, I covered my unfortunate friend with the sandy soil to rest there for ever by the river. Then, panic-stricken and in fear of my life, I made my escape through remote and pathless wildernesses; and like a man with murder on his conscience I left country and home to embrace voluntary exile. And now I have remarried and live in Aetolia.'

That was Aristomenes' story. His companion, who from the start had remained stubbornly incredulous and would have no truck with what he told us, broke out: 'Of all the fairytales that were ever invented, of all the lies that were ever told, that takes the biscuit'; and turning to me, 'But you,' he said, 'to judge from your dress and appearance you're an educated man – do you go along with this stuff?' 'Well,' I said, 'my opinion is that nothing is impossible and that we mortals get whatever the Fates have decided for us. You, I, everybody, we all meet with many amazing and unprecedented experiences, which aren't believed when they're told to somebody who lacks first-hand knowledge of them. But I do, I assure you, believe our friend here, and I'm most grateful to him for diverting us with such a charming and delightful story. Here I've got to the end of this long and rugged road without effort and haven't been bored. I believe my horse too thinks you've done him a favour, for without tiring him I see I've reached the city gates transported not on his back but, you might say, by my ears.'

That was the end both of our conversation and of our companionship, since they now turned off to the left towards a nearby farm, while I went into the first inn I saw and questioned the old woman who kept it. 'Is this town Hypata?' I asked. She nodded. 'Do you know somebody called Milo – one of your foremost citizens?' She laughed and said: 'Yes, you could call him foremost all right – he lives right outside the city wall.' 'Joking apart, mother,' I said, 'tell me, please, who he is and where he lives.' 'Do you see those windows at the end there,' she replied, 'that look outwards towards the city, and on the other side a door giving at the back on to the neighbouring alleyway? That's his house. He's enormously rich, with money to burn, but he's a public disgrace, the lowest kind of miser, and lives in total squalor. He's a usurer on the grand scale and only accepts gold and silver as pledges; he shuts himself up in that tiny house and broods over the corroded coins that are his ruling passion. He has a wife to share his miserable existence, but his whole household consists of one slave-girl, and he always dresses like a beggar.'

This made me laugh. 'It's a really good turn my friend Demeas did me when I set out on my travels,' I said, 'giving me an introduction to a man like that. At least I needn't fear annoyance from kitchen smokes and smells!' So saying I walked on and came to the door of the house, which I found firmly bolted. I proceeded to bang on it and shout, and at last a girl appeared. 'Now,' she said, 'after all that energetic knocking, what security are you offering for a loan? You must be aware that the only pledges we accept here are gold and silver.' 'God forbid,' I said; 'what I want to know is whether your master is at home.' 'Yes, he is,' said she, 'but why do you want to know?' 'I've got a letter for him from Demeas of Corinth.' 'Stay where you are,' she said, 'and I'll tell him,' and bolting the door again she disappeared. Presently she reappeared and unbolted it, saying: 'He says, come in.'

In I went, and found him reclining on a very small couch and just beginning dinner, with his wife sitting at his feet. By them stood a table with nothing on it, and indicating this, 'Welcome to our guest,' said he. 'Thank you,' I said, and gave him Demeas' letter, which he read quickly. 'I'm most grateful to my friend Demeas,' he said, 'for sending me so distinguished a guest,' and making his wife get up he invited me to sit down in her place. When I modestly hesitated, he pulled me down by the tunic, saying: 'Sit here. We are so afraid of burglars that we can't provide couches or proper furniture.' I did so, and he went on: 'I should have guessed rightly that you were of good family from your gentlemanly appearance and your – if I may say so – virginal modesty, even if my friend Demeas hadn't told me so in his letter. So, please don't despise my humble shack. There's a bedroom just here where you'll be decently accommodated; enjoy your stay with us. By honouring our house with your presence you'll enhance its reputation, and you'll be following a glorious example by putting up with a humble lodging and so emulating the achievements of the hero Theseus after whom your father is named – he, you remember, didn't despise old Hecale's frugal hospitality. Photis,' he said, calling the maid, 'take our guest's luggage and stow it safely in his room, and then quickly get out of the store-cupboard some oil and towels for massage and drying, and anything else he needs, and show our guest the way to the nearest baths. He's had a long hard journey and must be worn out.'

Hearing this, and bearing in mind Milo's character and his meanness, I decided to get further into his good books. 'Thanks,' I said, 'but I don't need any of those things, which I always take with me on my travels; and I can easily ask the way to the baths. It's my horse that is the important thing; he's carried me well. Here's some money, Photis; please get him some hay and barley.' That done, and my things stowed in my room, I set off for the baths on my own; but wanting first to see about something for our supper, I made for the provision market. Seeing some fine fish offered for sale I asked the price, which was a hundred sesterces; I demurred, and got them for eighty. I was just leaving when I met Pytheas, a fellow student at Athens. Recognizing me with delight after such a long time he rushed at me and embraced and kissed me affectionately. 'My dear Lucius,' he said, 'it's ages since we last saw each other, not indeed since we left Clytius' class. But what are you doing here so far from home?' 'I'll tell you tomorrow,' I said. 'But what's all this? My congratulations – for I see you with attendants and fasces and everything about you that befits a magistrate.' 'I'm an aedile,' he said. 'I regulate prices; if you want to do any shopping here, I'll take care of it.' I declined the offer, as I had provided myself amply with fish for supper. But Pytheas, looking at my basket and shaking up the fish to get a better sight of them, asked: 'What did you give for this rubbish?' 'I had a job,' I said, 'to get the fishmonger to take eighty sesterces.'

When I said this, he immediately seized me by the arm and took me back again to the market. 'Who did you buy this muck from?' he asked. I showed him an old man sitting in a corner, and he began to upbraid him sharply in his inspectorial capacity. 'So,' he said, 'this is the way you impose on my friends and visitors in general, putting ridiculous prices on your rubbishy fish and reducing our town, the pride of Thessaly, to a barren wilderness by making food so dear. But you're not getting away with it: I'll show you how roguery is going to be checked under my regime,' and emptying my basket on the ground he ordered his clerk to tread on my fish and trample them to pulp. Then, pleased with this display of severity, my friend Pytheas sent me on my way with the words: 'I think, Lucius, that that old man has been properly put in his place.' Astonished and completely bemused by all this, I took myself off to the baths, deprived of both my money and my supper by the energetic measures of my sagacious fellow student. Having had my bath, I came back to Milo's house and went to my room.

The maid Photis now appeared, saying: 'The master is asking for you.' Knowing Milo's parsimonious habits I made polite excuses, saying that it was sleep rather than food I felt I needed to restore me after the wear and tear of my journey. This message produced Milo himself. Taking me by the arm he tried gently to make me accompany him; and when I hesitated and put up a mild resistance, he said: 'I won't leave the room unless you come with me,' backing his words with an oath. Yielding reluctantly to his persistence I was led to that couch of his and sat down. 'Now,' he asked, 'how is my friend Demeas? and his wife? and the children? and the servants?' I gave him all the details. Then he questioned me about the reasons for my journey. I told him all that. Then it was my home town, its leading men, the governor himself, that were the subjects of minute inquiries. Finally, realizing that, on top of the stresses and strains of my journey, the additional fatigue of this long conversation was making me nod off in the middle of my sentences and that I was so worn out that I was muttering disconnected words that made no sense, he at last let me go to bed. So, not before time, I escaped from this tiresome old man and the interrogation plus starvation that was his idea of entertainment; and weighed down, not with food but sleep, having dined solely on conversation, I went back to my room and surrendered myself to the repose that I was longing for.

Book II

In quest of witchcraft – meeting with Byrrhena – warned
against his hostess the witch Pamphile – makes love to
the maid Photis instead – dinner with Byrrhena –
Thelyphron's story – promises to contribute to the
Festival of Laughter – encounters and slays three
desperate robbers

The moment the sun put the darkness to flight and
ushered in a new day, I woke up and arose at once. Being
in any case an all too eager student of the remarkable
and miraculous, and remembering that I was now in the
heart of Thessaly, renowned the whole world over as
the cradle of magic arts and spells, and that it was in this
very city that my friend Aristomenes' story had begun,
I examined attentively everything I saw, on tenterhooks
with keen anticipation. There was nothing I looked at in
the city that I didn't believe to be other than what it
was: I imagined that everything everywhere had been
changed by some infernal spell into a different shape –
I thought the very stones I stumbled against must be
petrified human beings, I thought the birds I heard
singing and the trees growing around the city walls had
acquired their feathers and leaves in the same way, and
I thought the fountains were liquefied human bodies.
I expected statues and pictures to start walking, walls to
speak, oxen and other cattle to utter prophecies, and

oracles to issue suddenly from the very sky or from the bright sun.

So, spellbound and in a daze of tormented longing I went on prowling, though nowhere did I meet with the slightest trace of what I hoped to find. While wandering from house to house like some reveller out on the town, I found myself unexpectedly in the provision market. There I saw a woman passing by with a train of attendants, and hurried to overtake her. From her gold-mounted jewellery and the gold embroidery on her dress it was clear that she was a person of some consequence. Walking with her was an old man; the moment he saw me, 'My God,' he cried, 'it's Lucius for sure,' and he embraced me and whispered in the woman's ear something I didn't catch. 'Now,' he said to me, 'won't you come and greet your foster-mother?' 'No, really,' I answered, 'I don't know the lady,' and I hung back blushing and shamefaced. But she looked at me and said: 'Yes, he's his sainted mother Salvia all over – it shows in his breeding and modesty. And his looks – it's uncanny, he couldn't be more like her: moderately tall, slim but muscular, nice complexion, a natural blond, simple hairstyle, eyes grey but alert and bright, really like an eagle's, a blooming countenance, a graceful but unaffected walk.' And she went on: 'It was I, Lucius, who brought you up with my own hands – naturally, being not only related to your mother but having shared a common upbringing. Both of us are descended from Plutarch, and we had the same wet-nurse and grew up together in the bond of sisterhood. The only difference between us is one of rank: she made a brilliant marriage, I a modest one. Yes,

I'm Byrrhena: I expect you've often heard my name mentioned as that of one of those who brought you up. So you needn't hesitate to accept the hospitality of my house – or rather of your own, for yours it now is.' While she was speaking I had had time to recover from my confusion. 'My dear mother,' I said, 'I can't very well throw over my present host Milo, having no cause for complaint, but I'll do my best consistently with my obligation to him. Whenever I can find a reason for coming this way in future, I'll always stay with you.' Chatting like this we came after a short walk to Byrrhena's house.

There was a magnificent entrance-hall, with a column at each of its four corners supporting a statue of Victory. Each of these, wings outspread, appeared to hover without alighting on the unstable foothold of her rolling ball, which her dewy feet just brushed, not standing fixed but seemingly poised in flight. In the exact centre of the hall stood a Diana in Parian marble. It was a brilliant *tour de force* of sculpture: as one entered the room the goddess with flowing tunic seemed to be coming straight at one in her swift course, inspiring awe by her powerful godhead. To right and left she was flanked by hounds, also of marble. Their look was menacing, their ears pricked, their nostrils flaring, their jaws ravening, and if any barking were heard nearby, you'd think it came from those stony throats. The crowning achievement of this accomplished sculptor's craftsmanship was that, while the hind feet of the dogs were braced firmly against the ground as they sprang forward, their front feet seemed to be running. Behind the goddess there arose a rock in the shape of a grotto, with moss and grass and leaves and branches, vines here and shrubs there, a whole plantation in stone. From inside the grotto the statue was reflected back in all its brilliance by the polished marble. Round the edge of the rock there hung grapes and other fruits so cunningly modelled that art had outdone nature in making them seem real. One would think that when at the time of the vintage the breath of autumn had ripened and coloured them, they could be picked and eaten; and when one stooped to look at the spring which gushed out at the goddess's feet and rippled away in a gentle stream, one would think the hanging clusters were not only real in every other way but were actually moving. From the middle of the foliage there peered out a figure of Actaeon in stone with his prurient gaze fixed on the goddess, the transformation into a stag already begun; one could see both him and his reflection in the spring as he waited for Diana to take her bath.

As I was examining every detail of the group with the utmost enjoyment, 'Everything you see,' said Byrrhena, 'is yours'; and so saying she took the others aside and told them to leave us. When they had gone she turned to me, saying: 'My dearest Lucius, I'm terribly worried about you – for I look on you as a son and want to see you securely provided for. Do, I implore you by Diana there, do be warned by me: watch out for the wicked wiles and criminal enticements of that woman Pamphile, the one that's married to Milo, him you call your host. Never lower your guard. They say she's a top-class witch, mistress of every kind of graveyard spell. By merely breathing on twigs or pebbles or any kind of small object she can plunge the light of the starry heavens above us into the depths of Tartarus and primeval chaos. The moment she sees a handsome young man, she becomes possessed by his charms and has no eyes or thoughts for anything else. She lavishes endearments on him, moves in on his heart, and binds him in everlasting bonds of insatiable love. And anyone who won't cooperate or gets written off for not fancying her, she instantly turns into a rock or a sheep or some other animal, and some she simply eliminates. That's what I'm afraid of for you, and what I'm telling you to beware of. She's always on heat, and you with your youth and looks would be just what the doctor ordered.'

Byrrhena's words showed how worried she was for me. However, with my usual curiosity, directly I heard the magic word 'magic', so far from resolving to steer clear of Pamphile, I itched to enrol myself as her pupil and to pay handsomely for the privilege – in a word to take a running leap right into the abyss. So in a delirium of impatience I extracted myself from Byrrhena's embrace as if her hands had been manacles and bidding her a hasty goodbye I hurried off at speed back to Milo's. As I rushed along like a maniac, 'Now, Lucius,' I said to myself, 'watch your step and keep a cool head. Here's the chance you've dreamed of, what you've always wanted. You'll be able to enjoy wonderful stories to your heart's content. Never mind childish fears, get to grips with the thing bravely. Granted, you'd better keep clear of any amorous involvement with your hostess and religiously respect the virtuous Milo's marital couch, but Photis the maid – you can go all out to make a conquest of *her*.

She's a pretty little thing, likes a joke, and is no fool. Why, when you went to bed last night, how sociably she took you to your room, how sweetly she helped you into bed, how lovingly she tucked you up and kissed your forehead! You could see from her face how reluctant she was to leave you; and she kept stopping to look back at you. It may be risky, but I'll have a go at Photis, and good luck to us!'

While I was arguing the matter out with myself I had arrived at Milo's door, and proceeded, as they say, to vote with my feet. I found neither Milo nor his wife at home, but only my dear Photis. She was getting dinner ready: pork rissoles, a succulent stew . . . and – I could smell it from outside – a splendidly savoury pâté. She was wearing a neat linen tunic, with a bright red waistband seductively gathered up high under her breasts. Her pretty hands were engaged in stirring the pot with a brisk circular movement, to which her whole body kept time in a sinuous response, while her hips and supple spine swayed in a delightful undulating rhythm. I stood in amazement, my attention riveted, admiring the sight; and something else stood to attention as well. Finally I said: 'How prettily, darling Photis, you're stirring that pot, and what a jolly rearguard action! That's a delicious stew that you're cooking! It'd be a lucky chap with nothing more to wish for in this world that you allowed to dip his finger in there.' To which the witty little baggage answered: 'You stay away, right away, from my little hearth, or it'll be the worse for you. You've only to be touched by my tiniest spark, and you'll take fire and burn deep down inside you – and nobody will be able to put out the flames but me. I know all the best recipes, and I'm equally good at keeping things on the move in the kitchen and in bed.'

As she said this, she looked at me and laughed. But I lingered there to drink in every detail of her appearance. As to the rest of her, I've nothing to say: it's only a woman's head and her hair that I'm really interested in. It's what I like to feast my eyes on first in the street, and then enjoy in private indoors. There are good and positive reasons for this preference. The hair is the dominant part of the body: it's placed in the most obvious and conspicuous position and is the first thing we notice. The rest of the body achieves its effect through brightly coloured clothes, the hair through its natural sheen. In fact most women, when they want to show off their personal attractions, discard their clothes altogether and remove all covering, eager to display their beauty naked, and reckoning that rosy skin will please better than gold fabric. If on the other hand – though it's blasphemy even to mention it, and I devoutly hope that such a thing will never happen to make the point – if you were to despoil the head of even the most beautiful of women of its hair and rob her face of its natural adornment, though she had come down from heaven, though she had been born from the sea and reared among the waves, I say though she were Venus herself, escorted by her choir of all the Graces and the whole tribe of Cupids, wearing her cestus, fragrant with cinnamon and dripping with perfumes – if she were bald, not even her Vulcan would love her. Then there is the fascination of its colour and sheen: now vivid enough to outshine the rays of the sun, now gently reflecting them; or varying its charm as its colour varies and contrasts – sometimes bright gold shading down into pale honey, sometimes raven-black with dark blue highlights like those on the necks of doves; or when, perfumed with Arabian essences and delicately parted, it is gathered behind to give back to the lover's gaze a more flattering reflection; or again when it is so abundant that it is piled high on top of the head, or so long that it flows right down the back. In a nutshell, hair is so important that whatever adornments a woman may appear in – gold, jewels, fine clothes – unless she's made the most of her hair, you can't call her properly dressed. As for my dear Photis, it wasn't that she had taken great pains with her hairstyle – it was its casualness that was so fetching. Her luxuriant tresses were carelessly flung back, hanging down her neck and over her shoulders; where they just touched the upper edge of her tunic she had gently looped them up and gathered the ends together into a knot on the top of her head.

I couldn't stand this exquisite agony of pleasure any longer, and leaning over her I planted the most honey-sweet of kisses just where her hair began its climb to the top. She turned her head, and looking at me sideways with fluttering lashes, 'Steady on, youngster,' she said, 'that's a bittersweet morsel you're sampling there. Watch out that too much sweet honey doesn't bring on a chronic case of acidity.' 'I'll risk it, sweetheart,' I said; 'just refresh me with a single kiss, and I'm all ready to be spitted and roasted over that fire of yours,' and so saying I hugged her tight and began to kiss her. By now her passion was beginning to match and rival my own;

her mouth opened wide, and her perfumed breath and the ambrosial thrust of her tongue as it met mine revealed her answering desire. 'This is killing me,' I said. 'I'm really done for unless you're going to be kind to me.' Kissing me again, 'Keep calm,' she said, 'I feel just the same, and I'm all yours, body and soul. Our pleasure shan't be put off any longer; I'll come to your room at dusk. Now that's enough; go and prepare yourself, for it's going to be a non-stop battle all night long, with no holds barred.'

After a few more endearments of this kind we parted. Midday arrived, and there came from Byrrhena a welcoming present in the shape of a fat piglet, five pullets, and a flagon of vintage wine. 'Look,' I said, calling Photis, 'here's Bacchus come of his own accord as Venus' supporter and squire. We'll drink every drop of this tonight; it'll put paid to any shyness or backwardness on our part and tune our desires to concert pitch. When one embarks for Cythera the only provisions one needs for a wakeful voyage are plenty of oil in the lamp and wine in the cup.'

The rest of the day was taken up with bath and dinner; for I had been invited to take my place at my friend Milo's elegant table and sample his delicate fare. Remembering Byrrhena's warnings I avoided his wife's gaze as much as I could, dropping my eyes before hers as if in fear of the bottomless pit. However, I kept encouraging myself by glancing over my shoulder at Photis, who was waiting on us. When evening began to fall, Pamphile looked at the lamp and said: 'We'll have a cloudburst tomorrow'; and when her husband asked her how she knew she just said that the lamp had predicted it. Milo laughed at this, saying: 'That's quite a prophetess that we keep here, this lamp which observes everything that happens in the heavens from her stand – or should I say her observatory?'

At this I struck in. 'That's just the ABC of this method of divination,' I said. 'In fact it's not surprising that this little flame, though it's produced by human agency, has divine foreknowledge of what that greater celestial fire is going to bring about in high heaven and is able to communicate it to us, being, so to speak, its offspring and sharing consciousness with it. Why, at this very moment there is a Chaldean staying in Corinth, where I come from, who's throwing the whole city into turmoil by his wonderful oracles, and publishing the secrets of Fate to all and sundry for cash down. He'll tell you the best day for making a lasting marriage or building a wall that won't fall down, the most suitable for business, the safest for a journey, the most appropriate for a sea voyage. When I asked him how this trip of mine would turn out he told me all sorts of different things, all equally marvellous: that I should win a brilliant reputation and become a legend, an incredible romance in several volumes.'

Milo smiled. 'What does this Chaldean of yours look like?' he asked, 'and what's he called?' 'He's tall,' I said, 'and rather dark-complexioned. His name's Diophanes.' 'That's him,' said Milo, 'the very man. He came here too and uttered a great many prophecies to a great many people. He did quite well, indeed he made a very tidy thing out of it, but then he unfortunately came into collision with Fortune in her most perverse, or rather adverse, mood. He was issuing his predictions one day in the middle of a dense crowd of bystanders when a businessman called Cerdo came up wanting to know the best day for a journey. He got his answer, and had taken out his purse, produced his money and counted out a hundred denarii as the fee for the prophecy, when a fashionable young man came up quietly behind Diophanes and twitched his cloak. When he turned round he found himself embraced and affectionately kissed. He kissed the young man back and asked him to sit down beside him; and being taken completely aback by this sudden arrival forgot the business he was engaged in. 'I've been expecting you,' he began; 'have you been here long?' 'Only since yesterday evening,' the other answered. 'But tell me, my dear fellow, how your land and sea journey went after you had to leave Euboea in such a hurry.'

'At this our worthy Chaldean Diophanes, still confused and not master of himself, "It was frightful," he answered, "positively Ulyssean – I wouldn't have wished it on my worst enemy. The ship we were on was so battered by storms and winds from every quarter that she lost both her rudders and was driven on to the further shore, which she just made before sinking. We lost all our possessions and had to swim for our lives. Then everything that charitable strangers and kind friends had contributed was taken from us by a gang of robbers; and when my only brother Arignotus tried to resist their violence, he was murdered before my eyes." Before he had finished this lamentable story, Cerdo swept up the money he had intended for the fee and left abruptly. Only then did Diophanes come to his senses and realize what he had lost through his lack of forethought, seeing all us bystanders doubled up with laughter. However, master Lucius, let's hope that our Chaldean told you the truth for once, and the best of luck to you for your journey.'

While Milo continued to hold forth in this vein, I was inwardly groaning, horribly annoyed with myself for having gone out of my way to start this series of irrelevant anecdotes, and so wasting a good part of the evening and its delightful enjoyments. In the end I said to him bluntly: 'Well, Diophanes must take his chance. I only hope that what he plunders from the public he again bestows in equal shares on land and sea. As for me, I'm still dog-tired from yesterday, so if you'll excuse me, I'll go to bed early.' So, saying goodnight, I left them and went to my room, where I found everything most elegantly arranged for our supper. Beds had been made up on the ground for the slaves some way from the door, to keep them from overhearing the sounds of our lovemaking. By my bed was a table with all the nicest left-overs from dinner, good-sized cups already half full of wine only waiting to be diluted, and the flagon standing by opened and all ready to pour – just what was needed to prepare lovers for the duels to come.

I had only just got into bed when Photis, having seen her mistress settled for the night, appeared smiling, with a wreath of roses in her hair and a bunch of blooms tucked in her breast. She kissed me lovingly, garlanded me, and scattered blossoms over me; then she took a cup of wine and pouring warm water into it offered it to me. Before I had quite finished it she gently took it from me and drank what was left in a most bewitching manner, sipping in minute instalments and gazing at me as she did so. A second and a third cup passed back and forth between us, followed by several others, until at last I was well under the influence. Mind and body alike were throbbing with desire, and finally I couldn't control the impatience that was killing me. Lifting my tunic for a moment I showed Photis that my love could brook no more delay. 'Have pity on me,' I said, 'and come to my rescue – fast. That war that you declared without any diplomatic overtures will break out any minute now, and you can see I'm standing to arms and fully mobilized for it. Since I got cruel Cupid's first arrow right in the heart, my own bow has been strung so hard that I'm afraid it's overstrung and may break. But if you really want to please me, let your hair down when you come to bed so that it flows in waves all over us.'

Without more ado she quickly cleared away the table and whipped off every stitch of clothing; then with her hair loose in delightful disarray she was prettily transformed before my eyes into Venus Anadyomene, shading her smooth femininity with her rosy fingers – more from a desire to provoke than to protect her modesty. 'Now fight,' she said, 'and fight stoutly; I shan't give ground or turn tail. Attack head on, if you call yourself a man; no quarter given; die in the breach. There'll be no discharge in this war.' Then climbing on the bed she let herself down slowly on top of me; and rising and falling at a brisk trot and sinuously rocking her supple body backwards and forwards she regaled me to repletion with the delights of Venus in the saddle, until exhausted and totally drained in body and soul alike we simultaneously collapsed, panting for breath, in each other's arms. In encounters of this kind we passed the whole night until dawn without a wink of sleep, from time to time resorting to the wine cup to reinvigorate ourselves, stimulate our desire and renew our pleasure. That was the pattern for many subsequent nights.

One day Byrrhena insisted that I should have dinner with her, and though I made all sorts of excuses she would not take no for an answer. So I had to go to Photis and as it were take the auspices from her. She was reluctant to let me out of her sight, but kindly granted me a short furlough from our campaign of love. 'But look here,' she said, 'mind you get back early. There's a gang of young idiots of good family disturbing the public peace just now. You can see murdered men lying in the open street, and the provincial police are stationed too far away to save the city from these killings. You're well off and an obvious target, and as you're a stranger they won't be bothered about repercussions.' 'Don't worry, Photis dear,' I said. 'Apart from the fact that I'd have preferred my pleasures at home to dining out, I'll set your fears at rest by coming back early. And I shan't go alone either. My trusty sword will be strapped to my side, so I shall be carrying the wherewithal to protect my life.'

So equipped and forewarned I went out to dinner. I found a large company there and, as you would expect in the house of such a great lady, the pick of local society.

The sumptuous tables were of polished citron-wood and ivory, and the generous wine cups were all alike valuable in their different styles of beauty. Some were of glass skilfully decorated in relief, some of flawless crystal, some of shining silver or gleaming gold or amber hollowed out with wonderful art, and there were gems to drink from – you name it, it was there, possible or not. Great numbers of footmen in splendid liveries were deftly serving one ample course after another, while boy slaves, curly-haired and prettily dressed, kept on offering vintage wine in cups fashioned from whole gemstones. Now the lamps had been brought in, and the convivial talk reached a crescendo, with hearty laughter and witty quips and pleasantries flying back and forth. At this point Byrrhena asked me: 'Are you enjoying your stay here? My own belief is that when it comes to temples and public baths and buildings of that kind we needn't fear competition from any other city, and as for basic necessities we have all we want and more. The man of leisure can relax here, while the man of affairs will find all the bustle of Rome; and the visitor of limited means can enjoy rural seclusion. In fact, we're the pleasure-resort for the whole province.'

'Very true,' I said; 'and I don't think I've ever felt freer anywhere than I have here. But I really dread the dark and inescapable haunts of the magic arts. They say that even the dead aren't safe in their graves, but that their remains are gathered from tombs and funeral pyres, and pieces are snipped from corpses in order to destroy the living; and that at the very moment of the funeral preparations old hags of sorceresses will swoop down to snatch a body before its own people can bury it.' To this another guest added: 'Round here even the living aren't spared. Somebody we know had a similar experience which left him mutilated and totally disfigured.' At this the whole company burst into helpless laughter, and everybody's eyes turned to a man sitting in the corner. He was put out by this unwelcome attention and muttering indignantly got up to go. 'No, do stay for a bit, my dear Thelyphron,' said Byrrhena, 'and like the good fellow you are tell us your story again, so that my son Lucius here can enjoy your agreeable and amusing tale.' 'You, dear madam,' he answered, 'are always kind and considerate, but some people's rudeness is intolerable.' He was evidently upset, but when Byrrhena persisted and pressed him, unwilling though he was, to tell his story as a personal favour to her, he eventually did as she asked.

So having piled the coverlets into a heap and reclining half upright on one elbow, Thelyphron stretched out his right hand like a man making a formal speech, with the third and fourth fingers bent, the other two extended, and the thumb raised slightly as if in warning, and began. 'I had not yet come of age when I left Miletus to see the Olympic games. Then I wanted to visit this part of your famous province, and so after touring all over Thessaly I came in an evil hour to Larissa. My money was running low, and I was looking round the town in search of some remedy for my poverty, when I saw in the public square a tall old man. He was standing on a stone and loudly announcing that if anybody was willing to watch a corpse, he would negotiate a price. "What's this?" I asked a passer-by. "Are corpses here in the habit of running away?" "No, no," he said. "A mere boy and a stranger like you obviously can't be expected to realize that this is Thessaly you're in, where witches regularly nibble pieces off the faces of the dead to get supplies for their magic art."

'"But tell me, please," I said, "about this business of watching over the dead." "First of all," he said, "you have to stay wide awake for the entire night; you mustn't close your eyes for a second but must keep them firmly fixed on the body. You mustn't let your attention wander or even steal a sidelong glance: these dreadful creatures, who can change themselves into anything, will take on the shape of any animal you like to name and creep up on you in stealth – it's no trouble to them to outwit the eyes even of the Sun or Justice herself. They can take on the forms of birds or dogs or mice or even flies. Then they lull the watchers to sleep with their infernal enchantments. There's no end to the tricks that these vile women contrive to work their wicked will. But the fee for this deadly job isn't as a rule more than five or six gold pieces. Oh, I nearly forgot: if the body isn't intact when it's handed over in the morning, whatever's been removed or mutilated has to be made good from the watcher's own person."

'Having taken this on board, I summoned up my courage and went up to the crier. "You can stop shouting," I said. "Here's a watcher all prepared. Name the price." "You'll get a thousand sesterces," he said. "But look here, young fellow: this is the son of one of our chief citizens who's died, and you must guard his body faithfully against the evil Harpies." "Nonsense," I said, "don't give me that rubbish. You see before you a man of iron, who never sleeps, sharper-eyed than Lynceus or Argus, eyes all over him." I had hardly finished speaking when he took me straight off. The house to which he brought me had its front door closed, and he ushered me in through a small back door, then into a shuttered room where he showed me in the gloom a weeping woman in deep mourning. Standing by her, "Here's a man," he said, "who has engaged himself to guard your husband and is confident he can do the job." She parted the hair that hung down in front to reveal a face that was beautiful even in grief. Looking at me, she said: "Please, I beg you, do your duty with all possible alertness." "You need not worry," I said, "just so long as the fee is satisfactory."

'Agreement reached, she rose and took me into another room. There was the body draped in snow-white linen, and when seven witnesses had been brought in she uncovered it herself. After weeping over it for some time she invoked the good faith of those present and proceeded to call off meticulously every feature of the body while one of the witnesses carefully wrote down a formal inventory. "Here you are," she said. "Nose all there, eyes intact, ears entire, lips undamaged, chin in good shape. I ask you, fellow citizens, to note and attest this." The tablets with the list were then sealed and she made to leave the room. But I said: "Please, madam, will you give orders for me to be supplied with everything I'll need?" "What might that be?" she asked. "A large lamp," I said, "and enough oil to last until dawn, and warm water with flagons of wine and a cup, and a plate of left-overs from dinner." She shook her head. "You talk like a fool," she said, "asking for suppers and left-overs in a house of mourning where there hasn't even been a fire lit for days and days. Do you think you're here to enjoy yourself? You would do better to remember where you are and look sad and tearful." With these words she turned to a maid. "Myrrhine," she said, "make haste and get a lamp and some oil, and then lock up the room and leave him to his watch."

'Left alone with the corpse for company I rubbed my eyes to arm them for their watch, and began to sing to encourage myself. Dusk came, and darkness fell, and time wore on until it was the dead of night. My fear was at its height when there suddenly glided in a weasel which stood in front of me and fixed me with a piercing stare. I was alarmed at seeing this tiny animal so bold. "Get out," I shouted, "you filthy beast, get back to your rat friends before I give you something to remember me by. Will you get out?" It turned and left the room, at which moment I was abruptly plunged into a bottomless abyss of sleep; the god of prophecy himself couldn't have told which of the two of us lying there was deader, so lifeless was I. Indeed I needed somebody to mount guard over me, since I might just as well have been elsewhere.

'The crowing of the crested company was singing truce to darkness when I at last woke up. With my heart in my mouth I rushed over to the body with the lamp, uncovered its face and checked off all the features: they were all there. Now the poor weeping widow, in great anxiety, came bursting in with yesterday's witnesses and fell on the body, covering it with kisses. Then after examining every detail by the light of the lamp she turned and called her steward Philodespotus. Having ordered him to pay over the fee immediately to their trusty watchman, which was done then and there, she added: "We are most grateful to you, young man; and what's more, for this faithful service we shall from now on count you as a particular friend." Delighted at this unexpected windfall and spellbound by the shining gold, which I was now jingling in my hand, "Madam," I said, "count me rather as one of your servants, and whenever you need my services, don't hesitate to command me." The words were scarcely out of my mouth when the whole household, cursing the evil omen, fell on me with every weapon they could lay their hands on. One punched me on the jaw, another thumped me across the shoulders, and a third jabbed me viciously in the ribs; they kicked me, they pulled out my hair, they tore my clothes. So, bloodied and ripped apart like another Pentheus or Orpheus, I was thrown out of the house.

'While I was getting my breath back in the street outside, I belatedly realized how thoughtless and ill-omened my words had been, and admitted to myself that I had got off more lightly than I deserved. At this point I saw that the final lamentations and last goodbyes had been uttered, and the corpse had now left the house. As was traditional for a member of an aristocratic family, it was being given a public funeral. The procession was passing through the city square when there appeared an old man in black, weeping and tearing his handsome white hair. Seizing the bier with both hands he cried loudly, his voice choked by sobs: "Citizens! I charge you, as you are true men and loyal subjects, to avenge a mur- dered fellow citizen and punish this wicked woman as she deserves for her horrible crime. She, and no one else, to please her lover and get her hands on the estate, has poisoned this unfortunate young man, my sister's son." These tearful complaints the old man loudly directed now to this individual and now to that. The crowd began to turn ugly, the probability of the thing leading them to believe his accusation. They called for fire, and started picking up stones and egging on the street-urchins to kill her. She burst into tears (which were obviously rehearsed), and by all that she held sacred called on the gods to witness that she denied this awful crime.

'Then the old man said: "Suppose we leave the proof of the truth to divine Providence. We have here in Zatchlas of Egypt a prophet of the first rank. He has already agreed with me a large fee to bring back the soul of the deceased from the Underworld for a short while and restore his body to life." So saying he led forward a young man dressed in a linen tunic and palm-leaf sandals with his head shaved bare. Repeatedly he kissed the man's hands and touched his knees in supplication. "Have pity, O Priest," he said, "have pity by the stars of heaven, by the infernal powers, by the natural elements, by the silences of night and the sanctuaries of Coptos, and by the risings of Nile and the secrets of Memphis and the sistrums of Pharos. Grant him a brief enjoyment of the sun and let a little light into those eyes which are closed for ever. We do not seek to resist Fate or to deny Earth what is rightfully hers; we beg only for a short spell of life so that we may find consolation in vengeance." The prophet, propitiated, laid some sort of herb on the corpse's mouth and another on his breast. Then turning eastwards he silently invoked the majesty of the rising sun, arousing among the witnesses of this impressive performance excited expectations of a great miracle.

'I joined the crowd, and taking up a position on a tall stone just behind the bier I watched the whole scene curiously. The corpse's chest began to fill, its pulse to beat, its breath to come; it sat up and the young man spoke. "Why, why," he said, "have you called me back for these few moments to life and its obligations, when I have already drunk the water of Lethe and embarked on the marshes of the Styx? Leave me, I beg you, leave me to my rest." To these words of the corpse the prophet returned a sharp answer: "Come now, tell the people everything and clear up the mystery of your death. Don't you know that my incantations can call up Furies and that your weary body can still be tortured?" The man on the bier answered and with a deep groan addressed the people: "I died by the wicked arts of my new wife; doomed to drink her poisoned cup I surrendered my marriage bed to an adulterer before it had grown cold." At this the exemplary widow put on a bold front and began to bandy words with her husband in a blasphemous attempt to rebut his accusations. The people were swayed this way and that, some calling for this abominable woman to be buried alive along with her husband's body, others holding that the corpse was lying and should not be believed.

'However, the young man's next words put an end to their doubts. With another deep groan he said: "I will give you the clearest proof that I speak nothing but the truth, and I will tell you something that nobody else could know or predict." Then he pointed at me. "There is the man," he said, "who guarded my body. He performed his duties with the utmost alertness, so that the hags who were waiting to plunder my corpse, though they changed themselves into all sorts of shapes to achieve their purpose, failed to outwit his vigilance. At last they wrapped a cloud of sleep round him, and while he was buried in deep oblivion they kept calling me by name, until my numbed limbs and chilled body made reluctant efforts to obey their magic summons. But at this point he heard his own name, which is the same as mine, and being in fact alive, though sleeping like the dead, got up without knowing what he was doing and like a lifeless ghost walked mechanically over to the door. Though it had been carefully bolted, there was a hole in it, and through that they cut off first his nose and then his ears; so he suffered the mutilation that was meant for me. Then, so as not to give the game away, they made shapes of his missing ears and nose in wax and fitted them exactly in place. And there he stands, poor devil, paid not for his work but for his disfigurement." Horrified at what I had heard, I started to feel my face. I took hold of my nose, and it came off; I tried my ears, and so did they. Everybody was pointing at me, turning round to look at me, and there was a roar of laughter. Bathed in a cold sweat I slunk away through the crowd, and since then I've not been able to face returning home to be mocked, looking like this. So I've grown my hair long to hide my missing ears, and my shameful nose I keep decently covered with this linen pad.'

Directly Thelyphron had finished his story the guests again broke into drunken guffaws. While they were calling for the traditional toast to the god of Laughter, Byrrhena turned to me. 'Tomorrow,' she said, 'we have a festival which is as old as the city and unique to us, when we propitiate the god of Laughter with happy and joyful ritual. That you're here will make it even more agreeable. It would be nice if you could provide some witty diversion in honour of the god that would enhance our celebration of his great power.' 'Right,' I said, 'I'll do as you ask. I'd love to devise some suitably lavish adornment for this great god.' Then, reminded by my servant that night was coming on, and having by now had more than enough to drink, I got up and with a brief good-night to Byrrhena began to make my way unsteadily home.

But no sooner were we in the street than the torch on which we were relying was blown out by a gust of wind, leaving us hardly able to see our way in the sudden darkness and stubbing our toes on the stones in our fatigue as we continued on our homeward course, holding on to each other as we went. We were nearly there when suddenly there appeared three strapping fellows who hurled themselves violently at our front door. Our arrival, so far from deterring them, made them redouble their attacks in competition with each other. Both of us, I in particular, naturally took it that they were robbers of the most savage description, and I at once drew from under my cloak the sword I had brought with me for just such an emergency. Without wasting time I charged into the thick of them, and taking on each in turn as he confronted me I buried it in him to the hilt, until at length, riddled with many gaping wounds, they expired at my feet. When the battle was over, Photis, who had been woken up by the noise, opened the door, and panting and sweating I dragged myself into the house, where, as exhausted as if I had slaughtered Geryon himself rather than three robbers, I fell into bed and passed out.